Saint, Sorrow, Sinner

The Gideon Testaments Book Three
Freydís Moon

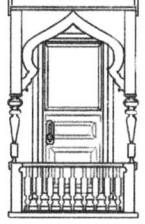

Copyright © 2024 by Freydís Moon

All rights reserved. ISBN: 9798872941170

Cover Artwork and Interior Illustration by M.E. Morgan

No portion of this book may be reproduced in any form without written permission from the publisher or author, except as permitted by U.S. copyright law.

Also by Freydís ☾

Exodus 20:3
Three Kings
With A Vengeance

The Gideon Testaments
Heart, Haunt, Havoc
Wolf, Willow, Witch
Saint, Sorrow, Sinner

Praise For ☾

Olivia Waite named *Heart, Haunt, Havoc* a New York Times Best Romance Book of 2023

"An enchanting conclusion to The Gideon Testaments, *Saint, Sorrow, Sinner's* religious horror and sapphic romance deftly weave together into a story that's bloody, rich, and tender."
—**Morgan Dante** author of *Providence Girls*

"Eerie as a haunting, biting as the midwinter night, and as tender as the ache of new love, *Heart, Haunt, Havoc* lingers long past the last page."
—**K. M. Enright** author of *Mistress of Lies*

"This capstone to the Gideon Testaments trilogy draws together its entire cast in a vivid, fast-paced haunting, where queer bodies are the brutal, beautiful flashpoint between predator and prey."
—**Rien Gray** author of *Double Exposure*

Content Note

Saint, Sorrow, Sinner contains sensitive material, including but not limited to: sexual content, body horror, animal death, horror, depiction of mania, discussion of sexual abuse, familial abuse, and religious abuse, bloody gore, drowning, depiction of panic, suicide ideation

Here is the repeated image of the lover destroyed.
Clumsy hands in a dark room. Crossed out. There is something
underneath the floorboards.
Crossed out. And here is the tabernacle
reconstructed.
Here is the part where everyone was happy all the time and we were all
forgiven,
even though we didn't deserve it.
Inside your head you hear
a phone ringing, and when you open your eyes you're washing up
in a stranger's bathroom,
standing by the window in a yellow towel, only twenty minutes away
from the dirtiest thing you know.
All the rooms of the castle except this one, says someone, and suddenly
darkness,
suddenly only darkness.

Richard Siken

Chapter One

Sophia gripped the edge of the vanity, staring at her distorted reflection in the steamy bathroom mirror, and listened to the house on Staghorn Way erupt. Someone huffed, exhaling through a frustrated groan. Another person rambled, out of breath and strained—*wait, wait, Bishop, put that down. Hold on, so . . .*

The witch spoke like a seedy politician. "Look, I don't expect you to be *thrilled*, but it's done, okay? I did what I did and—"

"Lincoln integrated with a demon, Tehlor! ¿Qué chingado?"

"And he's my problem now," she snapped. "Put on your big brujo pants, because we've got wolves sniffing at our door and they're a lot meaner than that one."

"Don't *point* at me." Sophia recognized his voice: the wolf-man who conjured fire. She tipped her head toward the open doorway, listening. "If you kill me, you kill her," Lincoln said. A chair scraped the floor. Footsteps beat, slow and steady. "Your call, Bishop."

"Okay, that's enough." *Stranger*. Sophia narrowed her eyes and held her breath, straightening in place. "Can we—"

"You crossed the line," Bishop interrupted.

Tehlor barked out a laugh. A single *hah*. "Oh, please. Get off your high horse, sweetheart—"

"*Enough.*" Palms connected. The sound cracked like thunder.

The celestial gong rattled Sophia's skull, panging in her chest, dizzying her. She flattened one hand on the countertop and caught herself on the doorframe with the other, enduring a harsh ripple of nausea. Blazing, hellish *heat* scorched her throat and sizzled the base of her spine. She shifted her focus to the blurry outline of her upper half. That noise, whatever it'd been, shot through her body like an arrow, reverberating from her forehead to her ankles. She inhaled deeply, staring at her button nose, heart-shaped face, cutting cheekbones, slender throat. Shared things. Points of recognition she'd once found in lost places. The longer she looked, the more she uncovered—Amy De'voreaux's bright eyes, straight teeth, perfectly plucked brows—and the more she saw, the harder it was to tear her gaze away.

The strange church bell faded, and the pain did, too, leaving whispers behind. Ghostly voices chittered between Sophia's ears. They surfaced when she slept, coasted through her mind on quiet mornings, and refused to let her rest. Right then, she caught the tail end of a tortured howl and the featherlight tickle of her sister's laughter on the edge of her jaw. She swallowed bile and hot saliva.

Downstairs, one of the newcomers said, "Now, tell us what happened." He paused to sigh. "In great detail."

The steam cleared and the muggy bathroom cooled. Sophia watched her fair beige skin appear, freckled and wholly plain, and tried to ignore the soft, purplish dents beneath each eye. So much like their mother, an unrefined version of her sister. She let go of the doorframe and brought her hand to the glass, watching familiarity bend beneath her fingertips. *Me,* she thought, convincing herself, *that's me, right?*

The witch, Tehlor, told the story, and the wolf-man, Lincoln, interrupted every fourth sentence. *We infiltrated a cult,* she said. *Haven,* he added. Sophia's skin reached for bone.

They described a mockery of worship. Pretending to praise God at church, casing the congregation's rental at the barbecue, and finding a young woman locked away on the second story. *The Breath of Judas.* Tehlor's voice darkened. *They were killing women, Colin.* The conversation muddled. *They were going to use her to—*

Each person became interchangeable, warped under an onslaught of sudden lightheadedness. *What're you talking about* and *Tehlor's not lying* and *what the hell did you two do?* Sophia's heart drummed hard. *You don't get it; you're not hearing me.* She pawed at a drawer, yanking it open. *Of course we wanted it for ourselves, but everything changed . . .* Her reflection shifted. She did not turn her head, but the thing trapped inside the glass did. Sophia choked on a sob. Willed herself to stay present, to remain in her body. *This wasn't some Heaven's Gate bullshit.* But the woman in the mirror had Amy's eyes, her blood-slicked smile, and wore their father's crucifix. Sophia grasped the handle on a pair of shears she'd found in the primary bedroom. *Don't look at me like that, Bishop. You weren't there.*

"One," Sophia's reflection sang. The poor rendition of Amy was stitched together by the chaotic energy shackling Sophia's soul. It was a puzzle upended and remade. Pieces missing. Not quite complete. "Two." Her cracked lips spread into a grin. Black streamed from the corner of her mouth. "Look at you."

Rose and Phillip were drowning them. Raping them, they were—

"Three, four . . ." Her raspy voice distorted, turning wicked and slow, like a sun-ripened record. "Baptize the whore."

Sophia brought the scissors to her long brown locks and snipped. She steadied her trembling hands, tried and failed to keep an ugly sob from echoing through the bathroom, and cut, cut, *cut.* The blade ran across the shell of her ear on a clumsy snip. Panic warred with the magic festering inside her. Somewhere deep; somewhere she couldn't reach. She exhaled through gritted teeth and aimed another harsh snap at her hair.

Get rid of it, she thought. *Gone, go, get it off me.*

Tehlor Nilsen, quiet as a wraith, appeared in the doorway and snatched her wrist.

Sophia froze. She thought of *Watership Down*, destruction and homemaking. Foxes, wilderness, and rabbits raised in hutches. She'd never met a woman like Tehlor before. She strained against the witch's hold, but Tehlor simply narrowed her eyes and squeezed.

"Where the hell did you find those?" Tehlor asked.

Fright sharpened into something else. Sophia tried to jerk away—mistake—and yelped when the taller woman pushed her backward, wrangling the shears out of her grasp. *Get away, run, stop.* She growled and squeaked but couldn't speak. Considered sinking her teeth into the soft, pale skin above Tehlor's sweater. She hissed instead. Clawed the same way she had when Haven initiates had taken her. Remembered calloused palms around her thighs, her sister's fingernails on her biceps, and Rose's perfume. She thrashed and swatted. Swore she was breathing but couldn't find any air. She gasped and swallowed, sucking in breath after breath, and still couldn't breathe.

"Hey, hey, whoa—okay, look at me," Tehlor said.

Metal on porcelain, *clank-click.* Soft hands. Warm too.

Tehlor gripped Sophia's wet cheeks and held her still. "Stop," she whispered, then again, pulling her full mouth around the word. *Stop.* "Breathe, Sophia." Tehlor inhaled deeply. Sophia followed. After three breaths, Sophia's vision stabilized. "Again." Tehlor exhaled. Sophia's heart rate refused to slow. She swallowed, tracking the glide of Tehlor's bony thumbs beneath her eyes, swiping at stray tears. "You're a fuckin' mess, you know that?"

"And you're a bitch," Sophia muttered, waterlogged and embarrassingly weak.

She offered a mean smirk. "A bitch who made you breakfast."

Sophia snorted. Burned toast and shitty scrambled eggs wasn't really breakfast, but she shrugged anyway. "I thought Lincoln did the cooking."

Tehlor rolled her eyes. A spotted rat sat on her haunches outside the bathroom, watching. When Sophia glanced at her, Tehlor said, "Gunnhild," like a teacher would to a student. "Where'd you find these?" Tehlor asked again. She dropped her hands from Sophia's cheeks and picked the shears up out of the sink.

"The big room." Sophia wiped her nose and sniffled.

"Did you go through my shit?" She arched a brow.

"Did you expect me not to?"

Clear, gray eyes sharpened. Sophia had spent the last two years avoiding people like Tehlor Nilsen. She'd seen women striding down sidewalks, laughing together inside cafés, buying discount groceries at the supermarket, but ferocity was something the second De'voreaux daughter had taught herself, and unrefined danger had never reflected back at her until right then. She swallowed hard, lifting her chin to meet Tehlor's harsh gaze.

"You're a murderer with a demon-guy on standby. You think I wouldn't find a way to protect myself?" Sophia added, rallying confidence.

Tehlor nodded slowly. She placed the shears beneath Sophia's chin, pressing the sharp tip against her throat. "And you think that demon-guy wouldn't kill you for less?" She offered a tired, playful look, one that said *c'mon, be for real*, and popped her lips, annoyed. She pulled the scissors away, gesturing to the toilet seat. "Sit down. Let me fix this hack job you started."

Sophia didn't move until Tehlor flapped her hands, waving the shears toward the toilet again. She sat on the lid and listened for movement or voices downstairs. Hushed chatter came and went, fluttering upward from the kitchen.

"Ariana Grande would bankrupt an orphanage for this kind of volume," Tehlor said. She raked her fingers through Sophia's wet mane. "What's with the haircut?"

I'm sick of looking like her. "Wanted a change."

"Uh-huh. And the panic attack?"

"What about it?"

Tehlor played with her hair, pushing it around, scraping her short nails across Sophia's scalp. "Happen often?"

"Couldn't say."

The witch hummed. She didn't sound convinced. "Well, you took off a bunch in the front, so it looks like we're doing a pixie or a mullet. Pick."

Sophia stiffened. Her cheeks flared hot. One time, a while ago, before Haven split from the Austin homestead, Amy had plucked wildflowers while they were on a walk near their parents' house and tucked the stems into Sophia's braid. Amy had told her about Daniel. *He's wonderful, and godly, and good, Sophia. He's just a little damaged.* And Sophia had ignored the bruise on her sister's wrist, shaped like a man's palm. She blinked away the burn behind her lashes.

"Mullet it is," Tehlor decided. "If you don't dig it, we'll chop it off and turn you into Tinker Bell. Hold still."

The shears made thick, blunt sounds as Tehlor snipped and shaped. Brown, wavy chunks fell across Sophia's socked feet, striping the fluffy bath mat. After a while, she closed her eyes, listening to Tehlor make pleased chirps, and anticipating the next snap of metal blades. When Tehlor told her to turn around, she did. And when the heaviest part of her locks gave way, she sighed.

"Are you going to kill me?" Sophia asked, so suddenly it startled her.

Tehlor stilled. She rested her slender hand on Sophia's shoulder. Silence filled the bathroom, and that long, dreadful pause curdled in Sophia's gut. But finally, the witch said, "No."

Another few minutes went by, quiet except for the snipping of scissors and the distant spray from the kitchen sink, until Tehlor set the shears down and pointed at the mirror. Sophia stood, stepping in front of the vanity to assess herself. *Different.* Thrill jolted through her. Her hair was short and choppy, sticking to her nape and curling away from her temples. Boyish, almost.

Tehlor scooped Gunnhild into her palm and leaned against the doorframe. "It'll look better when it's dry."

Sophia shifted her gaze to Tehlor's reflection, meeting her eyes in the mirror. They studied each other for too long, poised on opposite sides of an impossible conversation. Sophia remembered Tehlor at the revival, levitating, eyes milk-white, like a snake about to shed. How small she'd looked after that, heaped in the bathtub, barely breathing. She remembered Amy, soft as a hutch-raised rabbit, tender and easy to pull apart.

"Do you regret it?" Sophia asked, as if Tehlor could read her mind. Maybe she could.

"Is that what's goin' on your pretty little head?" Tehlor cinched her brow. A single tattooed finger followed Gunnhild's spine, stroking like a metronome. "The only thing I regret is forgetting your sister existed for long enough to let her stab me. If I could go back, I'd kill her first. Well, okay, not *first*. Second. Right after Rose."

Sophia had known liars her entire life, but she'd never met a liar like Tehlor. Someone so familiar with dishonesty that the act itself seemed second nature.

Tehlor rolled her lips and flared her nostrils, inhaling a deep breath. "They fucked you up, didn't they?"

Sophia recalled the exact moment Daniel's rib cage had snapped through his skin, bending like antlers. She'd wanted to wield that power, to break those bones, to be the last earthly thing he saw. But she'd plunged her hands—*corpse hands*—into her sister's stomach instead. Tore through to her core. Unmade her.

She flicked her eyes away from Tehlor and looked at her reflection again. "Who's downstairs?"

"Oh, we called a priest, actually. For the whole *portal to hell* thing you've got goin' on."

Sophia whipped toward her, teeth set, fighting the urge to make a fist or grab the shears.

Tehlor sputtered through a laugh. "Calm down, I'm kidding." She grimaced. "Sort of."

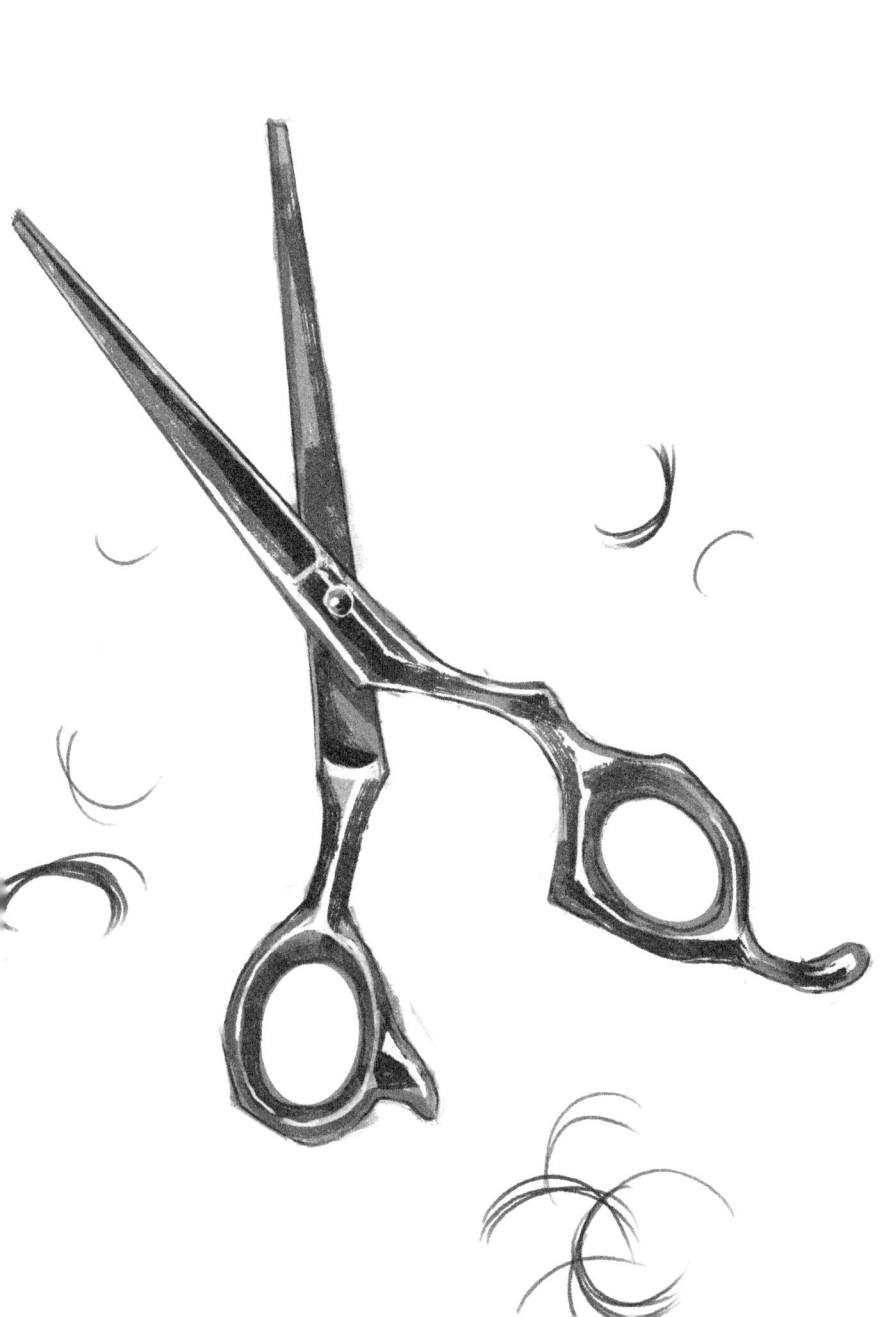

Chapter Two

S ALVATION WAS IDEALISTIC. SILLY, IMMATURE, and learned. But it was a concept Sophia understood, something she could tuck into tired places where defeat tried to burrow. She stood at the top of the stairs and prayed to a silent savior, repeating familiar thoughts like a comfortable tic. *Almighty, have mercy.* She pulled at the webbing between each finger and pushed her feet against the floor.

"Fear not, for I am with you. Be not dismayed," she whispered, swallowing the stone in her throat.

Sometimes she tested her own limitations for belief. Asked herself questions, nitpicked familiar verses, lashed out at Christ for his role in her abandonment. But no matter how often she invited doubt to take root, she knew one thing for certain: no creation could exist without its creator, and she'd already met the devil.

Okay. She pushed her freshly dried hair out of her face and slid her hand along the banister, descending the staircase one step at a time. A cinnamon-scented candle flickered on the table in the sitting room. An unfamiliar person stood next to the fireplace with their thumbs pushed through their belt loops and a holstered pistol strapped to their hip. At the mouth of the hallway, another newcomer made a soft, reverent sound, *ah-hah* but gentler. She gave him a once-over, glancing from his speckled brown socks to his fox face, narrow and studious, a handsome example of proper symmetry. Behind him, Lincoln stood at attention and Tehlor leaned against the back of the couch, cradling her rat.

Sophia switched her attention back and forth, watching the man in the hallway step forward while the person across from her adjusted their glasses.

"You're Sophia, right? I'm Colin." He rolled his sleeves to his elbows, exposing odd, angular tattoos scrawled across his fair skin. He smiled and shot a nervous glance at his companion. "Colin Hart. I specialize in hauntings—"

"He's an exorcist—"

"Bishop," Colin hissed, pursing his lips.

Sophia steeled her expression. She set her mouth and locked her knees, hyperaware of the gold crucifix seated on her sternum.

"I'm a brujo. She's a witch. He's . . ." They flexed their jaw. "Not supposed to be alive." Bishop lifted their brows and quirked their head, meeting her icy gaze. "What're you?"

The question stunted her. *What am I?* She shied away from the magic humming in her stomach, spreading like lichen.

"I'm nothing." She stared hard at Bishop. Gold bolted across their eyes, fast as lightning. "What's a brujo?"

"A spicy witch," Tehlor said, sighing. "Okay, look, they know everything, okay? They know about Haven, they know about the Breath of Judas, they know you're—"

"Being held against my will?"

"An accomplice," Lincoln rasped.

"A participant," Tehlor corrected. She saddled Sophia with a knowing look. "She controlled a corpse, remember? Tore big sis to pieces."

Lincoln hummed thoughtfully.

"Stop," Colin seethed, casting a hateful glance over his shoulder. When he turned back toward Sophia, he tried to smile. "Forgive me, those two have no manners." His eyes snapped to Bishop before he inched closer. "Neither does that one, apparently. Tehlor and Lincoln told us their version of events, but . . ." Another step. Close enough to make Sophia flinch. He stopped in his tracks. "Do you like coffee? Or tea, maybe?"

Sophia swallowed hard. "Tea, yeah."

"Good. Let's make some tea." Colin reached for her. It was a timid, reassuring touch, but the moment his fingertips met her bicep, something wild and destructive rose up and out of her.

No, she thought, *no, no, not again.* But the magic—if it was magic at all—lashed out, howling through her body, latching on to vertebrae and phalange, surging through her teeth, and temporarily stealing her sight. Her mouth yawned open against her will, and a sound manifested—one voice, many voices—until her own was silenced. She knew restraint. Had felt flesh and blood shackle her wrists the same way a ghostly presence kept her still right then. Had felt breath on her cheek, had known what it was like to become powerless.

"Rejoice, man of God. Blessed are those who honor the dead." The voice bursting from her throat was an axe splitting wood, and the terrible wail of betrayal, and a brutal, ugly sob. She tried to swallow it down, but it pushed upward, rolling across her windpipe. "Did the serpent spout legs and walk to Golgotha? Did he wield the spear? Tell me, Keeper of Seraphim, do you taste glory—"

Ringing, *ringing*, ringing. The high-pitched whistle after a firecracker popped, or a shotgun blasted, or cars collided.

Something clapped. Pain cracked through her face.

She came back to herself slowly, soul syrupy and liquid, slipping back into place. She blinked until her vision returned. *Don't puke.* Her bowels were loose and her stomach lurched. She sniffled, swallowing pennies and sulfur. *Don't pass out.*

Colin stood before her, hand clutched to his chest, opalescent eyes glinting. A halo crested his shoulders, turning his aura crystalline, and the black ink on his arms, hands, and neck stood higher. She could hardly bear to look at him, but she watched the shine fade from around his blown pupils and saw his mouth twist into a frown. The underside of her skin stung, and her gut clenched. Something echoed inside her. She felt like clay on a pottery wheel, scraped and reshaped. She shook her head and licked around her mouth, collecting irony slick from the grooves between her teeth.

"See," Tehlor chirped. "Told you."

"Fascinating," Colin muttered.

The room stopped spinning. Sophia shifted, righting herself against the lingering wooziness. Bishop hadn't moved from their place next to the hearth, but firelight flicked, causing a monstrous jaguar-shaped imprint on the wall to bend and shake. Shadowy ears twitched and a thick, spotted tail swept along the baseboard, leaving a trail of darkness behind. Their brown eyes shone treasure-gold. She inhaled through her nose and swallowed a mouthful of blood.

"Sorry," Sophia croaked.

"*I'm* sorry," Colin blurted, gesturing to her face. "Let me get you some ice."

She pawed at her cheek and glanced from Colin to Tehlor. She didn't trust any of them, but she'd coaxed the witch's heart to beat again, so she felt a sense of comradery with her. They'd seen each other die, sort of. Watched each other become unforgivable.

"Oh, he slapped you," Tehlor said nonchalantly, and shrugged. "Guess good ol' Iscariot isn't a fan of our neighborhood ghost-wrangling priest, huh?"

Colin parted his lips to protest but promptly closed his mouth. He nodded toward the hall, instructing Sophia to follow.

"How long have you been carrying the Breath of Judas?" he asked.

Sophia told her knees to bend, her feet to lift, and trailed Colin through the hallway. She tried to ignore the heat surrounding Lincoln, but as she brushed past him, something within her flared, yanking his hellfire closer. She remembered his molten hands—webbed with fiery fissures—tearing the clergy apart. Snow had turned to steam when it fell near him. She met his eyes. He laughed in his throat, an awful, knowing noise. *Holy Mary Mother of God, pray for us sinners,* she silently chanted, and tore her attention away.

Whatever brewed inside her recognized itself in Tehlor's bodyguard. She imagined a bushel of limbs pushing downward, smothering the Breath of Judas, but its magic bubbled between her imaginary fingers, sprang loose and stuck to her heart. No matter how hard she tried, the magic Haven had forced her to swallow would not budge.

"Sophia." Colin set the kettle on the stove. She startled, swiveling to face him. "How long has this been happening?"

"Few weeks," she said, clearing her throat.

"And how did it happen?"

Her vision wobbled. Panic needled her again. *Don't.* She glanced at Tehlor and shook her head. The witch lifted her brows and nodded. *Don't.* The memory was gluey in her mouth, brittle in her body.

"It's okay. We can skip that one. Can you tell me about Haven, then? Tehlor and Lincoln believe the pastor and his wife meant to impregnate the dead," Colin said. Disbelief cradled each word. "Seems a bit ridiculous, but—"

"Phillip and Rose were rebuilding the eighteen-year army," Sophia blurted. Her forehead tightened and she turned, looking between Tehlor and Lincoln. Hadn't they known? Hadn't they listened? She met their confusion with a huff. "Haven believed souls in purgatory could follow the dead back to their bodies. If they controlled who returned, they could start the rapture. Chosen vessels provided a birthright for the newborn and the reborn."

Tehlor's eyes bulged. *"Vessels?"*

"Yeah, vessels—heavenly hosts. Nine soldiers, eighteen saved."

Tehlor shot Colin a bewildered glance.

"Christ's eighteen-year lapse in the Bible," Colin said. He turned off the stove just as the kettle started to whistle and filled a mug. "Haven, like a few—*very* few—fringe pseudo-Christian establishments, believe Christ spent the unwritten time recruiting soldiers before he ever connected with his disciples. Some consider it a fail-safe; others believe it was removed by the Council of Mysia to preserve the integrity of the New Testament." He held the mug out to Sophia. "Correct?"

She took the mug. "Haven believed it was true."

"Do you?" He watched her carefully.

"I don't know."

"And they used you to, what, shove spirits inside corpses?" Bishop asked, stepping through the archway near the back of the kitchen. They grabbed a small basket and set it down on the table, sliding it toward her.

Sophia plucked an Earl Grey tea bag out of the basket and dunked it in her cup. *No,* she almost said, but it would've been half true. "Something like that."

Tehlor huffed. "Well, your sister told me Haven planned to kill—"

"They did," she bit out. Beneath her skin, everything buzzed and clenched. "Once they used the Breath of Judas to save nine soldiers and reanimate the eighteen-year army, they'd prosecute the betrayer." Tehlor opened her mouth, but Sophia kept going. "So, yeah, kill me," she deadpanned. "I know."

The witch listed her head. Annoyance tightened her mouth.

Lincoln propped his shoulder against the edge of the hallway. He gave Colin an unimpressed once-over. "You're the *specialist*. How do we get it out of her?"

Sophia surveyed the countertop. Before she could ask, Colin set a tiny, squirrel-shaped pitcher half-filled with milk on the table. She poured some into her cup and brought the hot drink to her lips. Steam dampened the tip of her nose. Lincoln's question loomed. *How do we get it out of her?* She turned toward the glass slider, tracking slow-drifting snow.

Four years ago, Sophia had given herself a deadline: December 26th. On that day, after she'd celebrated, and sang, and hugged her family, she would head north and start a life far away. But for four years, her deadline got pushed. *Next Christmas, I'll go. In a few months, Amy will be in a better place. By winter, I'll be ready.* Because for four years, when she thought of what she wanted, she always thought of her sister—occupied, caged, mistaken—and when she thought of her future, she always thought of her mother—bitter, alone, miserable—and when she thought of her faith, she always thought of salvation—promise, eternity, revelation.

So for four years, Sophia De'voreaux adapted a mantra of *soon, soon, soon*.

But Haven grew and split, and the congregation left Austin behind. Change felt like a blessing until Gideon became a curse.

I am no parasite, something said, sliding through her mind. Its voice oozed, thick and acrid. She sipped her scalding tea, attempting to drown it.

I should've left you. She thought of her sister. Remembered Daniel's calloused hands, pawing at her belt. *I should've run.*

Colin cleared his throat. "Unfortunately, this case is beyond me."

Snow kept falling. Sophia tipped the mug against her mouth. Tea scorched her throat.

"But I can make a call," he said, so softly she hardly heard him.

Sophia had never experienced the way winter settled over Gideon. Snow snapped at the window, frost scaled naked branches, and the bitter cold thinned every breath, making lungs work harder and blood run faster.

When she was small, she'd imagined playing in the powder, building snowpeople, making snow angels, letting snowflakes fall into her mouth. But being surrounded by ice-capped mountains was as brutal as it was beautiful, and she didn't know how much longer she could deal with the fucking cold. The house wheezed and creaked as midnight inched toward the witching hours. She tugged her sweatshirt over her hands, bundling the cuffs in her palms.

Seated on the edge of the bed, she stuffed the shears she'd found in the primary bathroom between torn denim and an old sweater inside a backpack Tehlor had loaned her.

If she left while everyone slept, she could walk to a gas station, or find a local shelter, or sneak onto a Greyhound and let it take her somewhere else. Preserve what remained of her life and find a nunnery willing to take a chance on her. Maybe join an intentional community looking for a baker. And if she didn't make it that far, maybe she'd die in a ditch on a stretch of desert road, become a halfway house for insects or a meal for a lone coyote. She remembered how Kimberly, the woman she'd reanimated at the revival, lurched back to life.

Would the Breath of Judas rile her body into movement too? Could she even *die* properly?

She glared at the backpack between a pair of too-big boots Lincoln had thrifted for her.

If she stayed, would one of the people in that peculiar house kill her to rid themselves of an inconvenience? Would the police arrive, asking questions about the corpses Tehlor and her hound abandoned in the forest? And if she ran, would she even make it out of Colorado? She raked her fingers through her hair.

"This is no different," she whispered, reminiscing on her four-year plan. "Grab the bag, stand up, go downstairs, leave. That's it."

Sophia glanced around the guest bedroom, zipped the backpack, and stood, creeping into the hallway. She hardly lifted her feet. *Where?* A voice erupted in her skull, hoarse and dusty. She did not answer—couldn't, really—because she didn't know *where*, didn't know *how*, didn't know a damn thing except for the unsettling urge to *get out*. She toed down the last two steps and sighed, stretching her arm toward the latch on the front door.

Before she could twist the lock, the porch lamp dimmed and flickered, fading until darkness spanned the front of the house. The hair on her nape stood. She held her breath. A bundle of light slid beneath the door, tumbled down the hall, and floated into an open palm.

Bishop, dressed in joggers and an oversize nightshirt, held a steaming mug in their free hand. Their mouth lifted into a smirk and the muted yellow lamplight stretched and twirled between their fingers, dancing.

They spoke softly. "Sneaking out?"

She set her teeth and gave a curt nod.

"Take something warm for the road," they said, and buckled their fist around the light, smothering it. They turned and padded into the kitchen.

Magician, someone whispered. The spirit spoke again, crying out behind her eyes. *Touched by the world-soul. Magician, magician, magician—*

Sophia pushed her thumbnail into her palm. If she left, she'd never know how a person like them could do a thing like that, so she set her backpack next to the door and followed Bishop into the kitchen. Moonlight beamed through the slider. With a flick of Bishop's wrist, an unlit wick on a candle labeled *French Patisserie* sparked to life on the table. They set a travel tumbler next to the candle.

"Sit down," they said. "You like cream, huh?"

"Sure, yeah," she said.

She tracked their lazy movements—opening the fridge, pawing around the shelves, knuckling at their cheek—and tried not to flinch when they set the carton down.

They rolled their eyes and huffed out a laugh. "Calm down, mija." They leaned their hip against the counter and offered a tired smile. "Hope you like chai."

"How'd you do that? With the light bulb, and the cat, shadow, *thing* . . . How'd you . . ." She exhaled sharply through her nose. "How'd you figure out how to control it?"

Bishop crossed the kitchen and spooned a dollop of honey into their cup. "Practice, mostly. Made a lot of mistakes. Gave too much of myself to someone I trusted and learned a hell of a lesson." They kept their distance, and she appreciated that, but the way Bishop carried themselves, so sure, so unbothered, scared her. They stirred their tea and met her eyes, nodding thoughtfully. "Eighteen?"

She cocked her head.

They mirrored her. *"Nineteen?"*

She snorted. "I'm twenty-one."

"You're full grown yet you followed a cult to Colorado," they stated, lifting their brows. Their smile twitched into a grin. "Did you drink the Kool-Aid or did somethin' else get to you?"

My sister. "I had nowhere to go." *I couldn't let Haven have her.* "So I packed my shit and went along for the ride." She pushed the taste of cardamom and chicory around in her mouth. *I wanted to believe.* "They weren't, like, an actual *cult* at first." The lie soured. She sipped more tea. "Maybe they were, I don't know." *I tried.* "By the time I wanted out, it was too late."

"How'd they convince you to go through with . . ." They lifted their pointer finger and gestured vaguely to her chest. "All that."

"Convince me," she repeated, and choked down a laugh. She kept her attention pinned to them. Maybe it was pride, maybe it was fear, but she refused to look away. "And I fight, not as one who beats the air, but I discipline my body and bring it into subjection." She watched for recognition, but Bishop merely blinked. "Amy recited scripture—that verse, specifically—when Rose baptized me."

"Drowned you," they said, not quite a question.

"According to an old Aramaic text, the Breath of Judas has to be administered at a crossroads. Life and death, purgatory, all that shit. My sister opened the vial, poured the"—she shrugged, clutching the tumbler until her palm sizzled—"whatever it was into her mouth and gave me CPR. I thought she'd saved me." *Forgiven me.* She cleared the anger clogging her throat. "So yeah. I wouldn't say they did any *convincing*."

Bishop nodded. "And now you've got your shit packed."

"What else am I supposed to do? Wait for one of you to pin the murder spree on me?"

They tipped their head back and forth. "Can't say I blame you for being paranoid, but that's not the plan."

"What *is* the plan, Bishop?" she asked. Their name echoed, hissed like a match strike.

"Look, I don't trust you either, okay? Let's get that out of the way." They sipped their tea. Their soft, round features and loose clothes were a confusing contrast to the shadowy jaguar that'd attached itself to their ankles yesterday. "I don't believe in much. Faith, maybe. Magic, somewhat. Power, obviously. People, though?" They shook their head. "But I just spent a good chunk of time watching Colin pull a demon out of a teenager. He saved that kid's life."

"And?"

"And I believe in him." They shrugged. "You'd be wise to believe in him too."

"Colin's the priest, right?" She slouched in the chair and glanced down the hall, staring at her backpack.

"Yeah," Bishop said, laughing under their breath. Something like love filled their voice. Hope, maybe. "He's the priest."

"And he has a friend in California? Someone who can help me?"

"I guess so."

Sophia faced Bishop again and brought the tumbler to her mouth, sipping gingerly. The question slipped out, accidental, quick. "Are you going to kill me?"

Bishop sighed. "No," they said.

A ghostly voice bloomed in her skull. *Liar.*

CHAPTER THREE

THE FIFTEEN-HOUR JOURNEY FROM COLORADO to Los Angeles left Sophia dazed and drowsy. She napped fitfully in the back seat of Colin's Subaru, dozing as the snow-capped Rockies disappeared in the rearview mirror. She woke once when they pulled into a truck stop for a bathroom break where she peed and stole a candy bar, and again as they motored through Moab, surrounded by stone arches and alien desert. Every so often she'd focus on the podcast Bishop had chosen for the road trip and flick back and forth between her text messages.

Before the revival, after Sophia's baptism, Sophia's phone had stayed in Amy's possession, tucked away in a pocket or purse, and handed over for supervised check-ins with their mother. *Holy vessels don't need electronics,* Rose had assured. *Best to stay unplugged.* She paused over the sunflower emoji next to Amy's contact information and tapped the name above it, opening her most recent conversation.

> **Tehlor Nilsen:** colin's a little cooky but he's nice

> **Sophia De'voreaux:** Is he going to exorcise me?

> **Tehlor Nilsen:** doubt it.

> **Tehlor Nilsen:** anymore nosebleeds?

Sophia tasted pennies. Back at the truck stop, crimson had poured out of her left nostril and dripped off her chin. A woman with two children had told her to tilt forward over the sink. *Everyone says to lean backward, but then you're just swallowin' yourself. Best to let it happen, sweetheart. Get it all out.* She'd set her palms on either side of the sink, watched herself hemorrhage in the mirror, and sniffled once it finally stopped.

> **Sophia De'voreaux:** Yeah.

> **Tehlor Nilsen:** just your nose?

She glanced at her fingernails. Thinner. Cuticles pink and peeling. She typed the truth—*no, it's spreading*—backspaced, then typed a lie.

> **Sophia De'voreaux:** Yeah.

Throughout the drive, Colin commented on Tehlor's truck appearing behind them, and when he thought Sophia was asleep, he lowered his voice and asked Bishop if they were making the right call. *We can't trust them, Bishop.* A sigh. Knuckles cracking. *Obviously, but this was the deal. You're the one who wanted to help her.* Tehlor had been her qualifier, her compromise, and if the witch hadn't tagged along, Sophia would've refused to go. She didn't know their four-sided history, and she didn't care to insert herself into whatever mess the group had made together, but she'd felt Tehlor's soul sputter like an old engine, and she recognized the careful way the witch moved around her. How everyone moved around the witch too.

Fear kept people at bay. Sophia knew that viscerally.

And everyone was afraid of Tehlor.

> **Tehlor Nilsen:** you doin okay?

Sophia read the message three times. She flicked the text bubble away and opened another, scrolling aimlessly through emojis, take-out orders, words of affirmation, and arguments. She stopped over a selfie Amy had sent before they left Texas. Faces smashed together, caught mid-laugh, eating vanilla soft serve on Halloween. They'd been talking about change, and growth, and God, and adventure. Amy had asked Sophia to bake her pumpkin bread. *The good kind with chocolate chips,* she'd said, and put her finger to her lips, signaling a secret. *Don't tell Rose. I'm supposed to do the keto thing with her. One little loaf won't hurt, though, right?*

Stability was a stolen thing for De'voreaux women and Sophia had never understood why Amy chose to make herself small instead of self-sufficient.

> **Sophia De'voreaux:** Do you think I should just lean in?

> **Tehlor Nilsen:** huh?

> **Sophia De'voreaux:** Should I just let it have me?

> **Tehlor Nilsen:** juicy question. probably not tbh.

> **Sophia De'voreaux:** Didn't you?

Three dots bounced. Disappeared. Bounced. Disappeared.

> **Tehlor Nilsen:** i let my gods have me.

> **Tehlor Nilsen:** judas isn't your god. plus i doubt that's actually him inside you.

A few seconds went by. Tehlor typed. Stopped. Started again.

> **Tehlor Nilsen:** and you don't wanna be like me, honey. i can promise you that.

What if I do? Sophia backspaced the question.

> **Sophia De'voreaux:** What if we can't get it out?

> **Tehlor Nilsen:** he might be the personification of a bible camp pamphlet but colin knows his shit

> **Tehlor Nilsen:** he literally exorsized lincoln. no joke.

Sophia read the text twice.

> **Sophia De'voreaux:** But this is beyond him, isn't it? That's what he said

> **Tehlor Nilsen:** give him a chance.

Sophia raked her teeth across her bottom lip and thumbed the text bubble away. Her lock screen was a stock photo of a dried garden rose. It reminded her of summer—youth, plastic pools, cheap ice pops, and Mom's flower bed next to the double-wide.

"Well, we're here. City of Angels," Colin said.

Bishop muted a podcast about Mesoamerica and blew out a deeply held breath. Palm trees striped the skyline. Change arrived in rapid succession, caged by concrete.

"It's big," she said, and leaned her forehead against the window, watching tall, gray buildings speckled with square windows dash by. Influencers armed with ring lights hurried down sidewalks. A long-haired young man played guitar on a corner, shoeless and accompanied by a leashed dog. Car horns honked, engines revved, shop doors opened and closed. Despite the flashy signs and brightly painted restaurants, the whole place seemed seedy and gaunt, buckling under too much weight. "Isn't Hollywood supposed to be, I don't know, more?"

"Movies make it pretty," Bishop said, shrugging.

Western Avenue met Santa Monica Boulevard, and they made a hard left into an adjacent neighborhood. Houses lined the cracked sidewalk, framed by short fences and neatly trimmed lawns. Some were small—older too—burdened with rotting porches and sallow paint. A few stood apart, bright and fanciful, entryways equipped with sleek keypads instead of doorknobs or dead bolts. As they drove, the neighborhood branched into segments, sheltered from the noise of the surrounding city.

"There it is," Colin said. He looped into a cul-de-sac and parked along the sidewalk in front of a peculiar alligator-green house.

Sophia tilted her head, studying the shingled roof and tall, round spire. She'd seen the same historical architecture in magazines. Beautifully painted shutters, honeysuckle busheled in garden boxes around the porch, roof angled sharply, pointing toward the sun. A copper placard on the fence read "Historic Site: The Belle House" and a neon sign—psychic readings—cast a pink glow across the window. It looked haunted. Dollish too. She half expected a guide to arrive and offer them a tour.

> **Sophia De'voreaux:** We just got here.

> **Tehlor Nilsen:** cool we'll be there soon. grabbing in n out. hungry?

> **Sophia De'voreaux:** Get me a milkshake

> **Tehlor Nilsen:** you need solid food.

"Tehlor and Lincoln will be here soon. They're stopping for food first," she said.

Bishop heaved a sigh.

"Well, let's get the initial introduction underway, shall we?" Colin glanced over his shoulder, offering a pained smile.

Sophia eased out of the car and flexed her calves. She pushed her hand through her hair and inhaled. Los Angeles smelled like exhaust and sunscreen, flora and cigarettes. The altitude in Gideon had sickened her at first, how thin the air had been. LA was low and coastal. Heavier, somehow. She filled her lungs, held on, and exhaled quietly, allowing the tightness in her chest to unspool. After Bishop and Colin exited the car, she followed the pair through the waist-high gate, across a neatly manicured stone path, and stepped onto the dark wood porch. She wrung her hands as the doorbell chimed and glanced from a stationary rocking chair to a matte black motorcycle parked in the driveway.

The door wheezed open.

"Colin Hart. It's been a long time."

Sophia turned, facing the stranger in the doorway. The woman spoke gently, voice warm and rich, and gave the priest a careful look. *You're not what I expected,* Sophia thought. Her paisley dress hit the floor, narrowly concealing a pair of satin slippers, and a finely knit cardigan drooped over one shoulder, exposing the long, lean line of her clavicle. Sophia drew her attention upward, focusing on the tilt of her brick-red mouth, and the expertly drawn daggers blackening each eyelid.

"Juniper Castle." Colin sighed her name. His smile fractured. "Too long, I think."

"You must be Bishop," Juniper said, turning toward them. She offered her hand. "Mucho gusto."

"Es un placer," Bishop said, and grasped her hand.

"She, her," she said.

They gave a curt nod. "They, them."

Juniper shifted her gaze, landing squarely on Sophia. "And you?"

Sophia opened her mouth. Closed. Opened again. The answer should've been simple. "She, her."

She hummed and crossed her arms, tapping a round, glossy fingernail against her cheek. Her eyes roamed, flicking around Sophia's face, then her torso, lower, all the way to her boots.

Colin cleared his throat. "Juniper, this is Sophia De'voreaux. Sophia, this is my colleague, Juniper Castle."

"Colleague." Juniper laughed in her throat. She shot Colin a playful look and stepped inside, propping the door with her foot.

The foyer opened to a staircase flocked with an ornate runner. Stained glass spanned the far wall, sending shards of colorful sunlight across the floor. To the left, vintage furniture filled a pastel parlor, and a crystal chandelier loomed above the entryway. Dark casing and wine-colored baseboards framed the interior, and haunting decorum hid in plain sight—gilded teeth glued to the edge of a lampshade, taxidermy mice posed like townsfolk on a cherrywood butler table, chunky crystals half buried with flourishing houseplants. The house smelled faintly of incense and citrus and seemed bigger than it appeared from the street.

Sophia left her boots next to the shoe rack beside the door and followed Juniper into the parlor. Her head swiveled, taking in the neatly bundled mesh curtains, mustard-yellow fringe sofa, and crowded bookshelves. Colin perused a round table in the window nook, stocked with tarot cards and an upright stone-carved palmistry hand. He traced the label on a lone manila folder.

"Working on something?" Colin asked.

Juniper eased her hand beneath his and took the paperwork. "Greyson's case," she said, and placed the file—*The Jericho Archives: Thirteenth Amendment*—in the table drawer.

"Those are *Vatican* archives," Colin said suspiciously.

Juniper offered a patient smile. "We're not here to talk about my brother." She looked at Sophia again, assessing her. "You're afflicted by magic, no? Spiritual warfare?"

Sophia blinked, taken aback. "I wouldn't call it *warfare*—"

"Make no mistake, it is," Juniper assured.

"And who are you, exactly? Another priest?"

"Obviously not," she said, lifting her brows. She tipped her head toward the sign in the window. "I speak to the dead."

Sophia switched her attention from Juniper to Colin. *For real?*

"I work from home," Juniper said. Her full mouth curved. She slid her gaze to Colin. "Give us a moment alone."

Colin immediately shook his head. "June, I'm not quite sure you've grasped the severity—"

"Colin . . ." Bishop cleared their throat. "C'mon, we'll fix some tea. I'm sure Juniper has a kettle."

"On the stove," Juniper said.

Sophia went rigid. Her skin sealed around her skeleton, and everything felt closer, trapped. The Breath of Judas shied away when she reached for it, coiling like a viper at the base of her skull. She wanted to open her mouth and shove her hand inside. Dig for it. Grab its tail and drag it out. She wanted to cough until it dislodged. Retch until the magic landed on her tongue. Pulverize it with her teeth; spit it on the floor. But she wanted to be alone with Juniper more. Wanted to know if Juniper Castle could truly communicate with the departed, wanted to see if this psychic could close whatever door Haven had opened. She met Colin's cautious stare and nodded.

The priest exhaled sharply through his nose. "We'll be in the kitchen."

He glanced over his shoulder and followed Bishop through a beaded curtain on the other side of the room, leaving Sophia alone with the mystic.

Sophia touched her thumb to each fingertip and chewed the inside of her cheek. She wanted someone to look through a microscope and see into her chest, her temple, her kneecap. She wanted someone to study her insides and find the malignance, tell her where to cut, how to open herself and remove it. She wanted intervention, she wanted—

"Psychic surgery is a popular practice in many spiritual circles," Juniper cooed. She inclined her head. Long black waves fell over her shoulder. "But I doubt it'd work."

Heat blistered in Sophia's cheeks. She'd snatched the word—*surgery*—from the forefront of her mind. Numbness crept from her hands to her elbows. Fright, maybe. Or thrill. "You're clairvoyant too?"

"It's not you I hear, Sophia."

The way her name filled Juniper's mouth, how the psychic's eyes narrowed. Sophia felt like a lamb in a slaughterhouse. She knew nothing, *nothing*.

"Your hitchhikers are loud," Juniper added, nodding slowly. "Can you hear them too?"

"All the time," she bit out. Her voice broke. "What do they want with me? Shouldn't I have some sort of control, some kind of"—she opened her hands, grasping at nothing—"power? Isn't that the whole point?"

Juniper shrugged off her sweater and draped it over the back of a velvet chair. When she stepped closer, Sophia flinched, startling. Embarrassment flared hot in her gut and her blush worsened. *Get it together*. She swallowed. *Stop acting like a goddamn bird.* "Sorry," Sophia blurted, bending her wrist to resist an unflattering movement. Recognition sparked—subtle flex, practiced resistance—and Juniper's confusion softened into something else. "I was never diagnosed." She tried to clamp her mouth shut, but the words were too thick to swallow. "Mom didn't believe in that shit, you know. Probably would've blamed the doctor for hinting at it."

"At what?" Juniper asked.

Sophia pursed her lips.

She took another step. "Autism?"

Sophia tried to nod but couldn't, so she thought *Yes, that, yeah*.

"I'm not surprised. Your sister brought you into Haven, no? Much easier for a trusted caregiver to manipulate someone who relies on authenticity—"

"I'm not stupid," she snapped.

Juniper closed the space between them and hooked her thumbs around the front of Sophia's ears. Her bony fingers disappeared into Sophia's hair, wrapped tight around her skull, and she angled her face upward, demanding eye contact.

"Didn't say you were," Juniper muttered. She studied Sophia down the curve of her nose. "You're like a little cat, you know that? Hissing and biting for no good reason."

That close, Sophia noticed the shallow lines around her upturned eyes and the dip beneath her bronzed cheekbones. Her lipstick feathered, spiderwebbing through tiny divots in her Cupid's bow, and an acne scar dimpled her jaw. She was beautiful, poised, and brave, and her hold on Sophia did not waver.

Again, Sophia thought of *Watership Down*. Rabbits, and cages, and hunters. *But first they must catch you.*

"She didn't trick me," Sophia said.

"Yeah, she did," she whispered, and it sounded like *obviously*.

Before Sophia could respond, the magic cowering near her nape lashed out, pushing against the underside of her skin. A ragged gasp tore through her. Vision, gone. Sound, muffled. The image of Juniper blinked in and out, moving like watercolors as the entity manifested. Like stepping into a coat, the spirit, ghost, *thing* slid into her arms, toed down her legs, and anchored itself to her feet. Sophia lurched against it. Jerked and spasmed.

Juniper sighed, digging her fingertips into Sophia's scalp. "Go on, then. Tell me your name."

Sophia's mouth shot open and a thousand voices poured out. She wanted to scream—*Sophia, I'm Sophia, Sophia De'voreaux*—but she couldn't find the strength to wade through the onslaught of ghoulish baggage. Every soul pressing against the membrane between her body and the living world brought grief, rage, hope, and desperation. She imagined they were a lake and tried to swim, smacking at slippery arms, pushing off shoulders, kicking at skeletal hands as they grappled for her ankles. Chased the glimmer at the surface, the promise of air, release, breakage.

"Sophia," she blurted, heaving in a deep breath. The voices rattled in proximity to her body.

Juniper dropped her hands. The frenzied spirits whispered and writhed, searching for a way out.

"Focus," the psychic said. "Come back."

Sophia swallowed stomach acid and blood. She followed Juniper's voice. *But first they must catch you,* she told herself, and repeated the quote like a mantra. *But first they must catch you, but first they must catch you, but first they—*

Quiet gusted through the house. Sophia jolted, righting herself against forced occupancy, and flexed her hands, feet, legs, spine, until her body became her own again. The sound of disrupted spirits lingered, echoing like a far-off farm bell. Manageable, though. Distant enough to ignore.

Juniper Castle stood before her, owlish and curious.

The beaded curtain swayed, clicking idly. Colin and Bishop clutched steaming mugs, wide-eyed and unmoving.

"Get her a towel," Juniper said.

Colin darted back toward the kitchen.

Sophia glanced at the wood floor and felt a bead of blood drip from her bottom lip, splattering in a small, dark puddle.

"What's inside me?" Sophia asked, hiccupping. Another mouthful of gore came up and out of her, stringing from her lips. She looked at Juniper through her lashes and wiped her chin with the back of her hand. Her knuckles came away red.

Juniper inhaled sharply. "Have you ever seen a seamstress unstitch two fabrics?" When Sophia shook her head, the psychic clucked her tongue. "Well, it's a lot like that."

"Here," Colin said, appearing at her side. "It's damp. I'll get you a dry one too. Are you . . ." He leaned closer, inspecting her. "Are you all right?"

No. But she didn't speak. Couldn't. *No, no, no.* She imagined a wedding dress torn in two. The unmaking of things—oil and water separating in a bowl, feathers plucked from a shrieking bird, the fluffy hide torn from a rabbit's body.

"She holds the unmade," Juniper said. The wobble in her voice betrayed her calm exterior. "And it is unmaking her."

Three knocks sounded at the door.

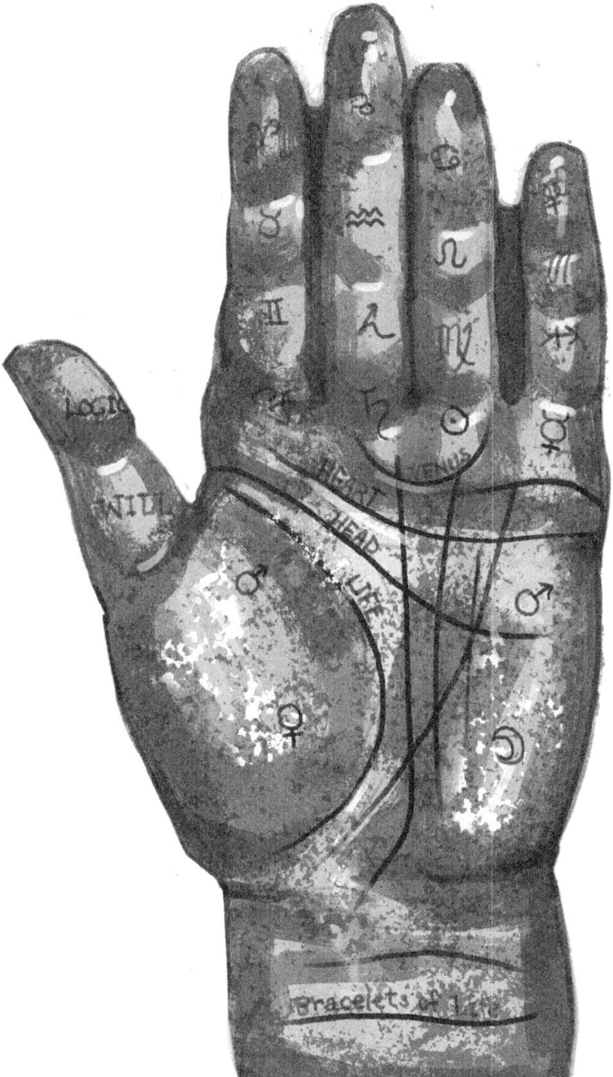
LOGIC
WILL
HEART
HEAD
LIFE
VENUS
Bracelets

Chapter Four

Sophia nursed a cup of chamomile tea and nibbled a cheeseburger. Tehlor watched her from across the kitchen, flicking her attention from the half-eaten sandwich to Sophia's face. Insistence and annoyance twisted her lips. *Eat,* Tehlor mouthed. The strawberry milkshake next to a basket of untouched fries was far more appealing, but the second she reached for it, Tehlor placed her hand on the lid and slid the cup away.

"Eat," the witch growled.

Like everything else in Juniper's house, the kitchen felt appropriately staged and entirely lived in. Vintage kitchenware and decorative appliances filled the counter space. Flowers bundled in burlap hung from a thin rope above the sink, and handwritten tags flagged each jar on the crowded herb rack. Colin and Bishop stood shoulder-to-shoulder next to the refrigerator while Lincoln leaned against the back door. Juniper stirred honey into a teacup, scraping the metal across thin porcelain. The sound hurt Sophia's teeth.

"There's a lot of unspoken happening in this house," Juniper said. She leaned against the doorjamb in front of the beaded curtain, staring into her cup. "You've brought a hellhound to my doorstep accompanied by the witch who stole him from the afterlife. A brujo out for blood," she hissed, snaring Bishop in a hard glare, "and an innocent vessel afflicted with religious magic threatening to unstitch the boundary between purgatory and our earthly plane." She sighed through her nose and raised her eyebrows at Colin. "Correct?"

Colin worried his bottom lip. "Quite jarring spoken plainly, but yes, that's correct."

"And you're responsible for the attack in Colorado." She looked between Tehlor and Lincoln. "Right?"

"Course not," Tehlor said, shrugging. She flicked her index finger between Juniper and Colin. "How do you two know each other? Thought the holy book axed friendship between godly men and"—she wiggled her fingers, grinning wickedly—"practitioners of the dark arts."

Colin jumped to speak, but Juniper cut him off.

"Colin attended the Sacerdos Institute with my cousin, Isabelle." Juniper's lipstick printed the edge of her cup.

Tension drained from Bishop's shoulders. They turned toward Colin, searching the priest's face. Behind her, Lincoln laughed.

"Incredible," the wolf-man mumbled, sarcasm thick over each syllable.

Sophia finished her burger and reached for the milkshake. Tehlor knuckled the cup toward her.

Colin cleared his throat. "Make no mistake, I wouldn't have brought this to you if I had another option."

"You've made their mess *your* mess," she said, inclining her head toward Bishop.

Colin's lips thinned. "Can you help her?"

"Saving one won't bring back the other—"

"June." Her name, familiar and changed, was a warning in his mouth, and for the first time, Sophia watched Colin's polished exterior give way to a far less put-together man. He huffed, exhausted. "What happened between you and I isn't hers to carry." He gestured to Sophia with his mug. "I knew the cost, I take the blame, I did what I did, Isabelle paid the price. She's gone; Sophia isn't. Now, can you help her? Or should I call Grey?"

Juniper lifted her chin. Defiance turned her statuesque, beautiful and cold.

No one said a word. Even Tehlor stepped away, shifting to stand behind Sophia's chair. She gripped her shoulders, an assuring touch, one sewed with compassion Sophia hadn't expected from someone so crass and deliberate. Gunnhild, her plump little rat, appeared between Sophia's feet.

"We can find someone else," Tehlor tested.

Sophia drank more of her milkshake, chasing sweetness, clinging to normalcy.

"No need," Juniper said. She inhaled a long, deep breath, and exhaled through her mouth. "Love is unassailable." Her gaze switched to Bishop, then moved to Lincoln, and finally came to rest on Sophia. "In its absence, we become insufferable. Given too much, we turn into gluttons." She paused, casting careful glances between each person. "I expect decency, respect, and good faith. Whatever you are to each other, whatever you've done to each other, put it away while you're here. Understood?"

Colin nodded hopefully, dancing his eyes around the kitchen, hunting for agreement.

Tehlor shrugged. "Sure, babe. You got it."

"Fine by me," Lincoln said.

Bishop, last to move, or blink, or breathe, finally relented. "Sí."

Juniper pinned them with a cool glance. "¿Me prometes, brujo?"

Their attention transferred to Lincoln. "Take your ring off."

The house stood still. Something old oozed, souring the air.

Lincoln tipped his head. He held Bishop's gaze as he worked the gold band over his knuckle and dropped it onto the table. The noise rang like a plucked harp string. Tehlor picked up the jewelry and tossed it. Bishop caught the band in one hand, turned it over like a hot coal, and tucked it into their pocket. Colin deflated.

"You have my word," Bishop said to Juniper.

"Good," Juniper said. The damage unspooled. Marginally, at least. The psychic sipped her tea. "Do you know what purgatory is, Sophia? Its true definition?"

"The place before Heaven," Sophia said. *Where you go to get clean.*

Juniper listed her head. An onyx curl tumbled over her shoulder. "It's the state of suffering. Expedited purification, so to speak."

Sophia narrowed her eyes.

Tehlor snatched a fry and chomped it.

"Imagine a thread binding two separate places, simultaneously holding them together and keeping them apart. One place—here—feeds the other—there—and if that thread ever frays or breaks, they begin to blend. The Breath of Judas is a tool, yes, but I don't think Haven realized what kind." Juniper traded her cup from one hand to the other. "See, most relics are of *use* to us, but this one . . ." She exhaled sharply. "This one grants the dead access to a crossing. *You* are the tool, Sophia."

"She's a ley line," Colin said quietly, as if he'd solved a riddle.

"Correct. I won't lie to you; this is unlike any possession I've ever seen. I'm sure Colin would agree." She waited for him to nod, then continued. "Ley line, yes—almost. But you're more like a house, I'm afraid." Her lips hovered apart, searching. "Haunted," she decided.

"Haunted," Sophia repeated. The word gusted out, small and fragile.

"There's a fissure inside you. Breakage like that..." Juniper paused, considering, and touched her sternum. "It isn't meant for us to carry. We're weak. Fragile. Unreliable. Imagine this magic is a ... a ..." She snapped her fingers. "Fungus. Like cordyceps, almost. I can feel it spreading. I can feel it ..." The psychic heaved a sigh. "Sprouting inside you, looking for new hosts. The Breath of Judas pushes out the living to make room for the dead. Anything it touches, it eats. And you're its primary host," she clarified. Her eyes softened. "So it's devouring you."

"We're dealing with zombie magic. Fine, cool, whatever. How do we get rid of it?" Tehlor asked.

"Scrubbing out spiritual rot isn't the same as evicting a wayward ghost. This is complicated," Juniper said.

"She's haunted, right? We have a cleaner." The witch jabbed her finger at Colin. "And a brujo, and a Völva, and a medium, and ..." She paused, gesturing with a limp wrist to Lincoln. "Sorcerer, demonologist—whatever he is. What's the holdup? Let's, I don't know, make Megazord."

Lincoln smothered laughter with his palm.

Sophia glanced over her shoulder. *"What?"*

"Power Rangers," Tehlor said matter-of-factly. She glanced around the kitchen. "It's Morphin' Time? C'mon, you can't be serious."

Juniper's plump mouth cracked into a smile. "Cute idea, but I doubt your particular gods would play nice. Mine won't, Colin's certainly won't, and ..." Her woodsy eyes darted to Sophia. "Do you pray?"

Fear not, for I am with you. Be not dismayed. Sophia nodded curtly.

"Who do you pray to?" Juniper asked.

God. The Holy Ghost. Whoever will listen. Prayer, as comfortable and sturdy as it was, had fallen on deaf ears for long enough to become a learned, empty, compulsive ritual. She'd gone to her knees and begged, called out for salvation in church, closed her eyes and asked God for strength. But Christ didn't choose her.

Haven did.

Who do you pray to? Rose had asked the same question not too long ago. Sophia still dreamed about it—crawling into an open mouth, down a throat lit with candles, and finding God inside the stomach of a starving beast. *The lion of the tribe of Judah.* She still dreamed about Daniel too. Bones erupting from his chest. Hands like iron around her wrists. The crushing weight of him; how he spoke through gritted teeth. *Is this what you wanted?* She picked her cuticle until Tehlor batted at her.

"Is that a garden?" Sophia asked, steering her attention toward a square of decorative glass above the back door. Beyond it, greenery brightened the horizon.

"It is," Juniper said, unfazed by the subject change.

Sophia didn't ask for permission, which she scolded herself for after abruptly standing and leaving the house, but she couldn't breathe very well. Couldn't cough up the sticky anger gumming her throat or shake the frantic chatter behind her left lobe. *Pray to who, pray to you, pray to him, pray to them, pray to her, pray to us, pray to us, pray to—* She rubbed her ear with the heel of her palm.

While the rest of the country decayed, winter closed around California like an expensive coffin, sheltering the landscape from decomposition. Palm trees speared the sky, birds sang, and honeybees floated around Juniper's garden, overgrown with vegetables, wildflowers, and herbs. Sophia sat in the grass with her back against a small, rectangular greenhouse. A flock of pigeons perched on a slouching power line, fluffing their wings, cleaning their feathers,

"You're a graveyard," Amy said, so clearly Sophia could've sworn her sister had manifested beside her. The spectral voice turned to steel, slick with venom. "Those who sleep in the dust will awaken. Let me out, let me out, *let me—*"

Something big and broad plopped in the grass. Sophia flinched, startling.

"Relax, kid. It's just me," Lincoln said, shaking out his wolfish head. His ears perked, and he licked his maw. Two-toned eyes scanned her face.

She rested the back of her head against the greenhouse and turned toward the birds. Lincoln did the same, following her gaze to the black wire. They didn't speak. *Thank God.* Truthfully, she was sick to death of talking. Sick of explaining, sick of reliving. A ladybug crawled over Lincoln's finger.

"I'm dying, huh?" Sophia asked.

"Yeah, I'd bet on it."

Finally. She sighed. *Someone honest.* "You wanted to use the Breath of Judas, didn't you?"

"Until I saw it in action." He shrugged, lifting the bug eye level. "Not very user friendly."

Sophia huffed out a bitter laugh. "Definitely not."

"What's it like?"

"Loud," she said. A pigeon twirled through the air, chasing a mosquito. "Like there's a thousand people inside me all trying to whisper through a keyhole."

"Gross."

"Did Tehlor actually bring you back from the dead?"

"Yeah."

"What's that like?"

Lincoln made a dismissive noise. "Bein' back? Same shit, different magic. But it's quiet for the most part. She's the loudest thing in here." He tapped his skull and jutted his muzzle toward the back door. "Bein' bound to a witch with a heart like a wildfire'll do that, I guess."

"You don't like it?" Strange to hear someone talk so flippantly about life after death.

"Being tethered to Tehlor?" He considered the question, smiling sheepishly. "I don't mind."

"Power," she clarified.

"That's subjective. Power is volatile. People steal it more often than they cultivate it. I made a deal for mine. Didn't go well." He shrugged. The ladybug lifted off his knuckle and flew into the air. "But once you get a taste of it—true power, I mean—it's hard to picture a life without it. Power like you have"—he tipped his head—"is a gamble. You can use it, be used by it, and hope you come out on top, or you can let it have you."

Sophia thought of cages again. Hutch rabbits and hunting hounds. "What would you do if you were me?"

"Rule the fuckin' world." The answer rolled off his tongue with practiced ease.

"Seriously."

"Fine, I'd *maybe* rule the world. I'd probably, like, retire, though. If we're being honest."

"We are."

"Then yeah. I'd retire."

"How?"

"Raise a corpse army, kill some politicians, storm a few banks, fill an offshore account, and settle down in a country with no extradition law. Pay an exorcist an ass-load of money to get the Breath of Judas out of me, buy Tehlor a nice house, and spend the rest of my life drinking fruity drinks on a white sand beach."

"I don't think I believe you," Sophia said. The wolf-man was too ambitious for such a cut-and-dried exit.

"If you would've asked me the same question last year, I would've meant it—taking over the world, having it all, hoarding power—but . . ." He gazed at the back door. His lupine ears twitched. "I can mourn the man I might've been and still appreciate who I'm becoming. I never thought . . . I don't know, I never thought I'd have *this*. I mean, c'mon." He scrubbed his palm over his furry head. "Not many people get a *third* chance. I used to want it all. Dying a few times changed that, I guess."

"But you'd still rob some banks," Sophia said, arching a brow. "Kill a few more people while you're at it."

Lincoln snarled a grin. "Oh, absolutely."

Sophia laughed and shook her head. When she looked back at the birds, she noticed a few had flown away.

Power. The word slithered through her, cooed like a lullaby. *What would you know of it, girl?*

Sometimes memories stole her voice. Sometimes they paralyzed her. Other times, she witnessed them from above, watching her past become small and conquered at the hands of Amy, and Rose, and Daniel, and Haven. *And Haven.* She sucked in the cool autumn air and reminded her lungs that they were not full of water.

"Sad, isn't it?" Lincoln pointed lazily at the power line. "Society domesticated pigeons ten thousand years ago, taught them how to carry mail, raised them as pets, and then rejected them once they weren't useful anymore. Now they're vermin. Rats with wings. Can barely make their own nests and still migrate to populated places because they're instinctually drawn to us." He yawned, stretching his maw, showing vicious, pointed teeth. "You ever think about that?"

"Pigeons?"

"People becoming gods. Training little creatures how to please us and then abandoning them once we've had enough."

Sophia thought of prayer, sacrifice, torture. Somewhere deep, buried where the Breath of Judas had chewed a hole through her spirit, something wicked and cold suckled at her inclination toward vengeance. Her heart clenched.

"I wanted Daniel dead," she admitted, so abruptly her vision went white. Panic brightened, immediate and blinding.

"Yeah?" Lincoln chuckled, impressed.

Her voice refused to surface. The confession, right there, burning on the tip of her tongue, wouldn't budge. *He held me down.* She swallowed. Restless spirits clamored toward the fissure inside her, pawing at her pestilence, prying at shadowy memories. *I'd never known violence until I found God.*

Lincoln Stone hummed deep in his throat. "Ah, yeah. Well, Tehlor pulled his whole rib cage out, sweetheart. I'm sure it hurt like a bitch."

Becoming the vessel will purify you, Amy had said, spitting the words at Sophia's feet. *Rose is sure of it.*

"I wanted him to suffer. There's something wrong with that, Lincoln. It's not . . ." *Holy. Godly. Graceful.* "It's ugly."

Lincoln snorted. "Deserved worse if you ask me."

"Who're you to judge—"

"He raped you, didn't he?" Lincoln spoke simply, easily, as if the violence had come and gone. Like it hadn't putrefied. Like she wasn't septic.

What's it like to be you, she wanted to ask. *What's it like to be feared?* When she tried to respond, her voice refused to surface, so she closed her mouth and waited.

"Deserved *a lot* worse," he said, and heaved a sigh.

"I became a monster," she whispered.

"Sometimes we have to."

"I didn't have to."

Lincoln shrugged. "Sometimes we want to."

Sophia swallowed around the truth. *Yeah, sometimes.*

"At least we're not them," he said, nodding toward the pigeons. "Abandoned and still hoping. That'd be brutal, wouldn't it? Stickin' around for love that'll never come back."

The rabbits became strange in many ways, different from other rabbits. Even to themselves they pretended that all was well, for the food was good, they were protected, they had nothing to fear but one fear. Sophia recited the quote to herself, reminiscing on soft paws, and turned soil, and the way her sister's palm had cracked across her cheek.

Somewhere close, Amy's ghost whispered about love, regret, sisterhood, and betrayal.

Sophia wanted her back. Wanted to kill her a second time, a third time. Wanted to apologize.

"Yeah, it would be," she said.

Sophia De'voreaux had never experienced a place as uncanny and charming as the Belle House.

After she'd followed Lincoln inside, the group agreed to get some rest before returning to the issue at hand—the Breath of Judas, Haven, her body becoming a tunnel between two worlds. Juniper had shown her to a room on the second floor with windows that looked out over the greenhouse and a Juliet balcony paired with elegant French doors, and Sophia had taken a shower in the bathroom across the hall, stocked with plum-scented soap and lemongrass lotion.

Hours later, she stood in borrowed nightclothes, listening to Bishop and Colin argue through the adjoining wall.

The couple talked about exorcisms, evildoing, and godhood. They both sighed like mules and spoke of consequences and judgment, religion and livelihood. *It'll kill her, Bishop.* Sophia pressed her ear to the wallpaper and squeezed her eyes shut. *You know it, I know it, everyone knows it. Sophia isn't long for this world. She'll die if we don't find a way to close whatever rift the Breath of Judas opened inside her.* The priest was a good, desperate man. His footsteps sent shock waves through the floor. *Tehlor said Sophia used magic at the revival. Necromancy or something like it.* Bishop's tone was sharp and brittle, verging on anger. *How do we know she won't harness that power again?* Sophia's throat went dry.

It's not power, she almost shouted, but kept her lips sealed. *It's not power, it's not power, it's not—*

She peeled her ear away from the wall, crossed the room, and stepped onto the balcony. Midnight cooled her feverish skin. The surrounding city sent an aurous glow into the sky, muting potential starlight. *Breathe.* She gripped the outdoor banister and tipped her head back, thankful for the breeze on her neck, and the inarguable sound of life. Tires rolling across asphalt, raccoons rummaging in a garbage bin, sirens blaring in the distance. That noise was real. Tangible. Far truer than the frantic chatter between her ears.

"But now, Lord, what do I look for? My hope is in you. Be not deaf to my weeping," Sophia mumbled.

The wind didn't stir. Heaven didn't open. An angel didn't appear with assurances of good news.

I hear you, someone said, voice shredded. Rose, maybe. *We'll keep you.*

Sophia would never know proper sleep again. She was sure of it. But she could get to know the house, at least. Make herself a cup of tea and explore the nooks and crannies she hadn't seen when they'd first arrived. She stared at the sky for another minute, willed the droning at the base of her skull to subside, then walked inside and made for the hallway.

The bedroom door clicked softly behind her. She lifted her heels and crept forward, flattening her palm on the wallpaper as she went. The staircase wheezed. Headlights winked through stained glass, illuminating a potted monstera beside the coatrack. Sophia traced the outline of the unlit neon sign in the window and glanced into the parlor room, scanning the round table for occult trinkets—*nothing*—then stepped backward into the hall, feathering her fingertips along the butler table.

Like this, the house presented itself differently. What was charming and decadent in the daylight became eerie and antiquated after nightfall. Oddities stood out in shadow. Rationally, she knew the taxidermy littered around the Belle House was, in fact, dead, but the darkness fooled her. If she looked hard enough, mice breathed, the bat pinned to the wall turned, and the pygmy deer mounted in the parlor twitched and shook. She thought about eternity, Eve, the tree of knowledge. Did Eden change after dark too? Did everything have a second skin, a second self? She pushed a short, wavy lock behind her ear. Did God create people to age, and change, and become different? Or did Moses carefully construct humanity of his own volition—rib bones, and nakedness, and innocence—as he wrote the Book of Genesis? Would God look at Earth and say *children*? Would he squint from afar and wade through déjà vu the same way Sophia padded through the Belle House, searching for recognition in a place she'd never been?

The scrape, turn, smack of a flipped card broke the silence. Sophia bristled.

That noise, the whip of thick paper, livened. She crept closer, following muffled voices, one clearer than the rest, toward a hidden inlet near the back of the solid staircase. Moonlight poured through the window, scaling a loose, gold rope, and deepened the shadowy gap between two velvet curtains. Sophia peered into the candlelit, windowless room and found Juniper Castle studying a tarot card.

"I require guidance, mother of ire, virgin of the forgotten, Mictlancihuatl," Juniper whispered. She set the card on a rickety table surrounded by floral wreaths and jarred candles. Cinnamon scented the air and patchouli smoke spun from an incense stick. A skeletal figure stood in the center of the altar, swathed in silk and lace, and bathed in firelight. "Santa Muerte, oye mí oración."

The psychic's oil-slick hair was roped into a neat bun and fastened with a scrunchie. She'd traded her paisley dress for a simple black tank and satin palazzo pants. Sophia carved her into memory—strong nose, sharp jaw, the slope of her throat, how her Adam's apple bobbed as she swallowed. Gold flickered on her brown skin, accentuating the dimples denting each cheek.

Beautiful, she thought, *like a bird of prey.*

Juniper curled her finger around the chain looped around her neck, playing absently with the charm. The pendant was oval, like most saint medals, but the image printed on its front was bony and unfamiliar. Sophia leaned closer, staring through the heavy curtains, and tracked Juniper's hand, the delicate press of thumb and index, as she plucked another card from the deck.

The image scrawled across the card featured two people holding chalices. The Two of Cups.

Does he speak and then not act? Sophia held her breath. The voice—ghost, spirit, *something*—came from within her, gentle and lilting, like a prayer for children. *Does he promise and then not fulfill?*

Juniper looked at the card and laughed. "No, no," she sang under her breath, and set it down, humming thoughtfully. "That can't be right."

Sophia focused on Juniper's palm, hovering above the deck. It wasn't until she leaned closer, strained to examine the fine details on the glowing altar, that she registered the stale breath on her face, or the anchor slowly lowering onto her sternum.

The moment Juniper laid her hand on the tarot deck, something sallow and half-gone lurched from the blackness. *Run*—shouted, screamed, sobbed. *Run*—echoing throughout Sophia's body, ricocheting in her skull, careening through her center. *Run!* It was Kimberly, the drowned woman from the revival, manifesting like a nightmare. The ghost snapped her jaws, chomping. *Run, run, run* forced past loosened teeth, and split lips, and blackened gums. *Run, run, run* choked, retched, spat. *Run, run, run* chanted like a spell, like a curse, like a warning.

Sophia jerked. Her knees gave out and she toppled to the floor. Panic spiked, red-hot and blinding. She swallowed the urge to scream and scrambled backward, gasping once her shoulders smacked the wall. When she whipped toward the curtains, Kimberly was gone.

Sophia couldn't shake the sight of the ghoul's open mouth, saliva stringing from her teeth, face corroded, distorted.

Juniper glared through the slot between the fastened curtains, clutching her Santa Muerte pendant. Her lips moved. *Sophia?* But no sound surfaced.

Run.

Sophia stumbled to her feet and darted through the quiet house. Her foot snagged the lip on the bottom step. She caught herself on the banister, reached for the crucifix strung around her neck, and squeezed the small, gold cross until her palm stung. Her lungs burned. Everything spun, brightening and dimming, blurring and sharpening.

Run.

She pulled herself up the staircase, ran down the hall, and locked the bedroom door behind her, sealing her back against it. The darkness threatened to swallow her, but she rewound the fresh memory once, twice, a third time, and focused on anything except Kimberly. Anything except the ghost. Anything alive.

Candlelight. Marigolds. Roses. Baby's breath. The tilt of Juniper's lips. How she smiled around the shape of Sophia's name.

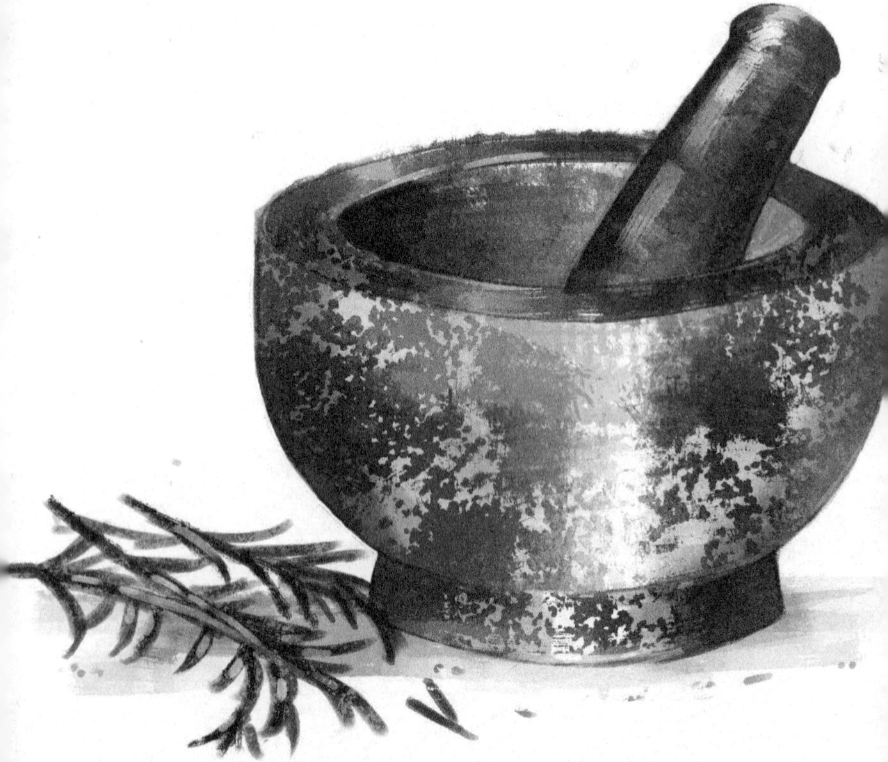

Chapter Five

Take my hand.

Walk with me.

What a garden, what a place, what a deception—

Sophia woke with a start.

Underneath each syllable, an old, refracted noise filled her skull. Throaty and guttural. Bellowing, trilling, moaning. *You sound like the ocean*, she wanted to say. *You belong in a museum.* It was prehistoric, reverberating from the ghost of a great, hulking thing. Sweat beaded on her forehead. Nightclothes clung to damp skin. Sophia hated recognizing such an irrevocable sound.

Extinction pressed against the chasm buried in her body, silent to everyone but her.

To hear the dead was to reach through time. Next, she might catch the echo of the great comet, or the pitter-patter of rain before the flood, or the slip of Eve's teeth against an apple.

Sleep came and went, shooed away the second Sophia opened her eyes. She didn't remember going to bed. Didn't remember anything except the dream—*was it a dream?*—replaying on a loop. Orange flowers, incense smoke, and Kimberly's snapping jaws. She stared at the ceiling and brought her hand to her chest, plucking at her father's crucifix.

Somewhere far away, she slid into another body. Pushed into cold, stiff skin the same way one might fit themself into a new glove. Heavy, dense bones. Atrophied organs. She stayed there for a moment, holding the gold cross, entranced by the incorporeal experience of possessing something, some*one* else.

Run, Kimberly snapped, lurching through her memories. The hand she should've called her own went taut, closing around the jewelry. *Run.* Sophia's breath shot from her, lungs suddenly seized, limbs suddenly shackled. *Run.* Death filled her mouth like curdled cream. She couldn't unlatch her knuckles from around the crucifix. Couldn't stop applying pressure.

Someone had taken hold of her. She wasn't inhabiting but being inhabited.

Sophia tried to yell. No sound surfaced. She tried to yank her hand away. Her grip tightened. Skin split. Bright, brilliant pain splintered. Blood welled in her palm.

"Let me go," she whispered, then again, rallying strength. "Let me go!"

The bedroom door swung open.

Sophia sucked in a sharp breath and shot forward, scrabbling off the bed. She extended her quivering hand, holding a small pool of warm blood, and lifted her gaze, staring at Tehlor Nilsen. Lincoln stood in the hallway behind her, peering over the witch's shoulder, and Colin's voice erupted from the bathroom, *what's going on out there,* while Bishop peeked around the doorframe.

Thick, syrupy blood filled Sophia's mouth. She swallowed it, ignoring the sticky rivulet dribbling down her chin.

"Something's inside me," she croaked. "Like, someone just . . ." She gestured to herself with her clean hand.

"Possessed you." Juniper's voice appeared before she did. The psychic touched Tehlor's biceps and stepped around her, striding into the bedroom. She tightened her satin robe and shook out her wrists, as if she'd swatted a spiderweb, before snatching Sophia's knuckles.

The movement jarred her. Sophia tried to yank away but Juniper tightened her grip. Blood smeared Juniper's hand, and her deep, chestnut eyes sparked. Gold veined her irises. Much like Bishop, the psychic exuded ancestral strength. Her hair rose, as if stirred by slow wind, and her lips moved around a soft, barely-there incantation. Her presence snuck into the tiny wound on her palm and flowed freely through her body, nipping at veins, marrow, and ligaments. When Sophia tried to retract her hands, Juniper made a disapproving noise. *Ah-ah,* like her mother.

"The dead are like mice," Juniper said. She slid her hand into Sophia's, aligning their palms. The blood between their skin spilled, stringing toward the floor. "They get trapped in the walls. Make noise at night. Chew through pipes and wires." Her energy was a comfort, intrusive and steady. "But once they've been seen, they go quiet for a while. They hide." She squeezed Sophia's hand and inched closer. Juniper's ethereal magic bent against bone, crept upward, climbed vertebrae.

All at once the noisy chatter hushed.

Sophia hiccupped on a laugh, halfway to an elated sob. "How'd you—"

"It isn't permanent," Juniper assured. She cleared her throat and unclasped their hands. The gore from Sophia's wound left a shiny crimson streak on her palm. "Get dressed. We'll talk downstairs."

Sophia glanced at the small puncture. Stigmata.

"I have bandages." Juniper tossed the statement over her shoulder and exited the room, brushing past the quartet of onlookers in the hall.

Gunnhild scampered across the floor and placed her small paws on the top of Sophia's left foot, blinking and twitching her nose. Sophia stared at the rodent while Tehlor said, "I got this," shooing Colin, Bishop, and Lincoln. Tehlor closed the door and folded her arms. A black long-sleeved dress clung to her small frame, paired with clunky heeled boots and an assortment of jewelry. She ran her thumb along an amethyst shard dangling from a silver chain.

"You okay?" Tehlor asked.

Sophia crouched and stroked Gunnhild's back. She'd never touched a rat before. "What does power feel like? Actual power?"

The witch shifted her gaze to the ceiling. Long wheatish hair fell over her shoulder. She hummed thoughtfully. "Control," she decided. "Sort of. Like, I wasn't completely *in* control at the revival, but I called the shots. Fenrir gave me the juice; I did what I wanted with it. Fast car, good driver. Loaded gun, skilled marksman. Make sense?"

"Do you think I could ever get that with . . ." She opened her unmarred hand. Gunnhild sniffed it then wandered back to Tehlor. She straightened, sighing at the sight of her bloodied palm. "Whatever's inside me? Is it even an access point, or a deity, or—"

"No, and no, and no," Tehlor said. "Sorry, honey. It's a curse. Point blank."

"Isn't a cure just a blessing sent with malice?"

"Yeah, and I don't think you want to find out what *malice* tastes like. My gods like me alive. The Breath of Judas needs you dead to survive. You do the math."

Sophia shifted her jaw back and forth.

"Power isn't pretty," Tehlor said, toeing at the floor. "C'mon, get dressed. I'll wait for you in the hall."

Once Tehlor left, Sophia gazed out the window, watching birds cut across the sky. She'd tasted malice at the revival. Knew the weight of it like an axe in her hand. A part of her wanted to wield it again. But the rest of her, the larger, morally sound majority, wanted to bury the woman she'd became at the first taste of revenge. She scrubbed the thought away while she dressed, sliding her legs into starchy denim and tugging a terracotta long-sleeve over her head. She stopped by the bathroom to fix her hair and brush her teeth.

The Belle House leaned into wakefulness the same way a youngling did. Like a kitten or a fawn, the place seemed to stretch, warming as its occupants puttered about. After Sophia turned the bathroom light off, Tehlor extended her arm, allowing her to lead the way.

Sophia crossed the hall, descended the staircase, paused on the last step, and turned toward the back of the house. Last night had been a dream, hadn't it? She caught the faint scent of decay—flowers, turning—and saw the yellow-gold rope tied around the curtains, cinching them shut. She remembered the sound—cards, flipping—and startled horribly when Tehlor touched her shoulder.

"Have you ever smoked before? Because a joint might help with"—Tehlor wiggled her fingers, flicking them down Sophia's body—"all that."

Sophia shot her an impatient glance, strode across the foyer into the parlor, and walked through the beaded curtain, joining the rest of the household in the kitchen. Bishop and Colin stood together next to the table where Lincoln sat, legs outstretched, arms folded. Juniper pawed through ingredients at the sink, uncapping a honey jar with one hand and grabbing a small wooden spoon with the other.

Juniper beckoned Sophia with a nod. "Honey is nature's greatest healer," she said, and opened her palm. Sophia stepped toward her and rested her knuckles on Juniper's hand. The psychic dolloped honey onto her damaged heart line, spreading the sweet, viscous syrup over the wound. "Who did you see last night?"

"What?"

"You saw someone. I did too. Who is she?" Juniper met her flighty gaze through long, painted lashes.

Sophia swallowed. "Kimberly, I think. She was Haven's first holy mother. Rose picked her."

"You *saw* her?" Tehlor seethed.

Juniper flashed her free hand, silencing the witch. "The Breath of Judas is a tether between two realities. Using it opens a mutual pathway. You're not controlling Kimberly anymore, but her corpse is still an unlocked door that something—or someone—could potentially crawl through." She wrapped a white bandage around Sophia's palm and yanked it tight, jostling her. "You're haunted, remember?"

Sophia gave a curt nod. "And you *saw* her?"

"I saw you too," she said, and arched a coarse brow. "Meddling is for mice, mija. No need to be a ghost in my home."

Heat filled Sophia's face. *So it wasn't a dream.* She set her teeth and brought her freshly bandaged hand to her side. Like an insect, wings pinned, encased in glass and carefully displayed, Sophia De'voreaux had become a specimen. Something to be exhumed, studied, and pondered.

"How do we close whatever Haven opened?" Sophia asked.

Juniper tsked. "*You* opened," she corrected, and stepped around her, reaching for the kettle. She fixed a cup of sencha and handed it to Sophia. "I'd like to perform a séance."

"A séance," Tehlor deadpanned.

Colin cleared his throat. "June—"

Juniper raised her voice and continued. "To contact whatever is attempting to occupy the marionette Sophia possessed at this"—she waved her hand in the air—"revival. If I can locate the breakage and assess the damage, we might be able to find a solution. Allowing the spiritual fissure to go unchecked will only make our problem worse, no?"

"She's a clown car full of ghosts," Tehlor said, gesturing wildly at Sophia. "You really think an open forum is a good idea? I'm not sayin' we shouldn't, but it could be one hell of a night if we aren't careful."

"We'll fortify the house," Juniper assured. "We're in a unique position. Five powerful practitioners sharing a common goal."

"Megazord," Tehlor said matter-of-factly.

Juniper's lips curved. "Sure."

"What's our fail-safe?" Lincoln asked.

Everyone turned toward him.

The psychic paused. "¿Perdón?"

He glanced at Sophia. "What's the plan if something goes wrong?"

Bishop's knuckles paled around the lip of the counter. "What *could* go wrong?"

"Given the situation? Anything," Colin said.

"If a ghost gets loose, I'll catch it," Tehlor said, shrugging. "Bishop and Colin, you'll focus on protection for Sophia and Juniper. Lincoln'll run defense." She pointed around the kitchen, jabbing at each person. "I keep what I catch, though, just so we're clear."

"Do you ever think about anything other than yourself?" Bishop snapped.

Tehlor clucked her tongue and picked idly at her nailbed. "I took care of your plants, didn't I?"

"Dios mío." Their chest emptied on an exhausted breath. "How could I forget?"

Juniper made a matronly sound. *Ah!* Sharp and raspy, aimed at Bishop, then chirped at Tehlor. *Ah!* She clucked her tongue. "No givin' ojo. You both agreed."

Tehlor smothered a laugh. Bishop rolled their eyes and gave Juniper a solemn nod.

Sophia swallowed a mouthful of grassy tea. "Okay, but what *is* a séance?"

"A séance is a courtyard. Anyone, friend or foe, can wander in or out." Juniper shrugged. "It's a place where we commune with the dead."

"And how will we *commune* with that dead when I'm a . . . a gateway, crossroads, vessel—whatever."

"Intention, prayer, energy." She sighed through her nose and gave Sophia a slow once-over. "You're a conductor. I'm a conduit. If all goes well, I'll pinpoint the place inside you that's in need of repair. Tehlor will collect any wayward entities, Bishop will keep me bound to this plane, and Colin will make sure you're safe throughout the communion." She flicked her gaze to Tehlor's spectral guard. He held his labradorite pendant between his teeth, leather cord dangling loose around his chin. Gunnhild perched on his shoulder, cleaning her snout. "Lincoln, you'll keep anything sinister at bay—that's your job."

"She's my job." Lincoln gestured to Tehlor with his coffee mug. The gemstone smacked his chest, flashing violet in the muted morning light. "If she's safe, you're all safe."

"Comforting," Colin muttered.

"What if something inside me is a threat to her?" Sophia asked.

Lincoln took a slow drink. "Don't let it out."

"Lincoln," Bishop warned. "Be reasonable."

"I'm being perfectly reasonable. Sophia's safety is your boyfriend's responsibility. No one wants her to fuckin' die, okay? But none of us know how this'll go and Tehlor's my—"

"Don't kill her, don't hurt her, don't let me die," Tehlor said to Lincoln. She lifted her arms in mock surrender and flashed a Cheshire grin. "There. Problem solved. Can we move on?"

Sophia turned her attention to Tehlor, searching the witch's face. Matte black lipstick, sharp eyeliner, dark mascara, but nothing bold enough to conceal the worry line between her brows. They looked at each other for a long time. Bound together by the moment they'd mutually seized—dodging death and embracing cruelty. Sophia wouldn't admit it, but she wanted to become her. Wanted to wield power with dignity. Laugh fully, love shamelessly, worship fearlessly. Being in Tehlor Nilsen's presence made conquest attainable.

"I won't let anything happen to you," Tehlor said, too quickly, like a secret spoken in plain sight, before her throat flexed, and she flashed another fake smile. "All right, we're havin' a séance. What's on the shopping list? I need jars."

Juniper flapped her lips. "I'll check my supplies; Sophia can text you. Colin, take Bishop to the carniceria. Short ribs," she said, pinching the bridge of her nose. "Chicken too. Bone-in."

Everyone traded confused glances.

"The living should *live* before connecting with the dead," Juniper said. She refilled her mug and replaced the tea bag with something new. "So we'll cook together." She shrugged, as if she'd said the simplest thing in the world. "Sustenance is a prerequisite to ritualism, isn't it?"

Evening fell over Los Angeles, but the Belle House stood alight in the darkness. Jarred candles flickered on windowsills, vintage lamps illuminated the parlor, and spices, oil, and herbs scented the crowded kitchen.

Flour dusted Sophia's palms. Her thumb left a soft white print on the stem of her wineglass. Cheap merlot soaked her bottom lip. If there was anywhere Sophia felt at home, if there was anything she felt overwhelmingly comfortable with, it was baking. The way tacky dough ballooned between her fingers, how individual ingredients came together for the greater purpose of creating something whole and new and entirely individual was a reliable ritual. She set the glass on the counter and ground the heel of her palms into a mound of fluffy dough, kneading until the uncooked bread was equally buoyant and sturdy. After, she gripped the rosewood handle on a well-loved dough cutter and separated the ball into individual lumps, rounding them with her palms. She sprinkled them with rosemary cut from Juniper's garden and drizzled Palestinian olive oil over each uncooked loaf.

"Look at you," Colin said, appearing at her side. "Quite the cook, huh?"

"It's my thing, I guess. I always thought I'd own a bakery." She placed the loaves onto a baking sheet and slid them into the oven.

The priest nodded reassuringly. "You will."

She offered a frail smile. Despite Juniper's psychic interference that morning, Sophia recognized the needle-sharp prick of unfamiliarity.

Felt the stirring of something alien and volatile growing in the back of her mind, like a roar of a distant storm barreling across blue skies. Next to the sink, Tehlor whined about ordering takeout—*pizza, beer, and buffalo wings would've been quicker*—while Lincoln diced onion and cilantro on a cutting board. At the stove, Juniper transferred rehydrated ancho chiles out of a bubbling pot and into a blender. Beside her, Bishop smashed avocados in a stone bowl. Lincoln carefully tipped the board over their mortar, spilling chopped veggies into chunky green paste. Bishop, curt and cold, said *thank you*.

Tehlor hoisted onto the counter and swung her legs. "All right, I know we haven't, like, eaten yet, but what's for dessert?"

"Chocolate soufflé," Sophia said.

"Soufflé? Teach me," Juniper said. The psychic gestured between the blender and Tehlor. "Would you mind? Blend, pour, stir. That's it."

The witch sighed and slid across the countertop, mumbling about *screwing it up* along with *don't blame me* and *I'm no fuckin' chef* while she reached for the blender.

Juniper stepped around Colin, dusting her hand across his shoulder as she went, and came to stand beside Sophia at the island. Her hair was fastened into a messy bun and her beige apron covered a black sweater paired with pleather pants. She smiled, assessing the ingredients strewn across the counter.

"Teach you," Sophia repeated. Nerves fired in different areas—spine, wrists, gums. She cleared her throat and nodded, arranging the ramekins she'd found in a drawer, and gestured to a clean bowl next to the flour sack. "It's, I mean, it's not *hard,* but it took me a few tries to get it right, you know, so, don't expect them to be—"

Gently, Juniper rested her wide palm on the small of Sophia's back. "Nothing perfect happens the first time. What can I do?"

Thumb against vertebrae. Heart line to tailbone. Sophia felt her everywhere.

Vocalization failed. She hummed, though. Tapped a flour-covered finger to her chin and realized where she needed to start. She opened the fridge, found the eggs, and handed one to Juniper. The psychic tracked her like a puma, orbiting every movement. When Sophia cracked the egg, Juniper did too. She separated the whites, dumping the yellow yolk into a smaller bowl, and smiled when Juniper said, "Ah, I see." Sophia chopped the dark chocolate while Juniper whisked the egg whites, and laughed when Sophia tilted her head, directing her to shake salt flakes into the darkening batter. For most of her life, Sophia pushed through the urge to stay quiet and spoke when speech was not a comfortable form of communication. But there, in the Belle House, surrounded by strangers who were becoming something else, Sophia listened, and smiled, and taught Juniper Castle how to bake a beloved dessert without saying much of anything at all.

Nearby, Tehlor laughed, and Bishop commented on the spiciness of the short ribs. Lincoln sipped from a beer bottle, hip propped on the edge of the sink, and Colin topped a salad with roasted pumpkin seeds. Days ago, she never would've thought the four could share a room, nonetheless a meal. But Lincoln pressed his mouth to Tehlor's cheek, and Colin adjusted Bishop's crooked glasses, and beside her, Juniper asked, "Do we chill the batter?"

Sophia nodded. *Yes.* She prefilled the ramekins with chocolate batter and slid them into the fridge. *You're beautiful, who are you, how did you—*

"Did your mother teach you?" Juniper uncorked the bottle of merlot and poured herself another glass. When she held the bottle out, Sophia nodded.

"She started to," Sophia said. Her voice was still hidden, crouching in the back of her throat.

Juniper—smart, attentive, poised—watched her lips. "My abuela taught me how to cook. She tried to teach me Spanish, too, but . . ." She shrugged, sighing wistfully. *"This is LA, Grandma. I'll be fine,"* she mocked, nasal and cute. She paused to laugh. Her smile waned. "Thought I knew best. I'm teaching myself, though. It's not the same, but it's what I've got. Qué remedio."

"When did you . . ." She paused, searching for the right way to ask a complicated question. "How did you . . . ?"

"Learn to speak to the dead? Oh, it's been . . . Twenty-two years, maybe? The women in my family are blessed with el óido—the hearing. So you can imagine the collective shock when *I* developed gifts." Her mouth split for another toothy laugh. "I ignored them at first. I think most of us do. But womanhood still found me. Rode to me, really, on the back of a botched ritual at a party in Pasadena."

Sophia pulled the bread from the oven and set the baking sheet on a cooling rack, glossing each browned loaf with honey butter. "Found you?"

"Isabelle found me, actually," she said.

Colin Hart shifted in place, averting his gaze to the tile. When Juniper held out the merlot, he extended his glass. His freckled face remained slack and open, but something brutal and finished slid through Sophia, reaching. *Isabelle.* She righted herself against it. Tried to ignore it. But the spirit refused to go unnoticed.

Take his hand. Isabelle appeared like a moth, like a sunflower, like a small, hopeful, fluttering thing. *Take his hand, take his hand, take his—*

When Sophia reached for him, the room stood still. The bustling kitchen tunneled inward. Time stretched. Movement, sound, light, everything paused, slowing like a faulty videotape. For a brief, significant second, Colin and Sophia were alone, suspended in their own private space. She slid her fingers around his palm and squeezed.

Love was finite like that. Offered freely at the behest of a ghost.

The touch lasted a heartbeat, no longer, and neither Colin nor Sophia knew what to do with it. *There,* she thought, aware of the house, the magic, the people around them, caught in the orbit of a stolen goodbye. When Sophia let him go, Colin chased her. She clutched her wrist to her chest. Once it was over, the reality they'd momentarily escaped came rushing back. Tehlor's raspy laughter. Lincoln snapping the cap off another bottle. Bishop taking Colin's chin, steering his face. *You okay, babe?*

Sophia blinked, hyperaware of her socked feet on the tile, and dishes clanking on the countertop, and a drawer rolling open.

Juniper flipped the dial on the stove, killing the flame. "When a spirit you love returns to you, it's hard not to listen. My cousin told me what I'd already known, what I'd kept hidden for a lifetime. Choosing to believe her meant finally believing in myself."

"She loved you," Sophia said absently. The thought consumed her until then, until she made it known. As quickly as Isabelle had arrived, slipping into her consciousness like a coil of smoke, she disappeared.

"She did. And I loved her," Juniper said. "Colin did too."

"How did she . . ." She paused, tripping over compulsive intrusion. "Sorry, I—"

"Exorcism is risky," Juniper said, shrugging. She stirred the steaming pot, filled with short ribs, vegetables, and spices, and gathered a bit of broth on the edge of her spoon, lifting it to Sophia's mouth. Sophia parted her lips, darting her tongue across curved wood. Sour lime, smoky cumin, fiery habanero, rich tomato. "It doesn't always go how we hope. Too spicy?"

Broth beaded at the corner of Sophia's mouth. Juniper swiped it away and sucked the sauce from her thumb.

"No, it's fine—*good,* it's good. I'm—I don't mind spicy," Sophia blurted.

Blistering heat climbed her sternum and settled in her cheeks. *Get it together,* she thought, scolding herself. *This woman is beyond you.*

"Good," Juniper said. She took a plate and handed it to Sophia, then passed another to Colin, Bishop, and so on. "Let's eat."

The group took turns spooning rice, meat, guacamole, and bread onto their plates and sat together at the table. With the leaf extended, there was just enough room for six. Sophia drizzled crema and homemade salsa verde over her ribs and dusted the rice in salt and pepper. She broke a piece of the loaf away and dunked it into broth and smashed avocado. Across from her, Colin made the sign of the cross and whispered *amen*, and Bishop rolled up their sleeves. Pillar candles flickered in the center of the table, hollowing Tehlor's cheekbones, and Lincoln hummed appreciatively as he tasted the sauce off his fingertip. Juniper hung her apron and took the seat beside Sophia.

"I've been on this planet for thirty-five years. All that time, and I think *this* is the strangest dinner party I've ever hosted," Juniper said. She propped her elbow on the table, cradling the bottom of her wineglass.

"Stranger than that ghost-hunting crew from Massachusetts?" Colin asked, pleasantly surprised.

"Oh, absolutely. They were exhausting, sure, but this is different."

Tehlor drizzled salsa over her plate. "Bet TLC could make us famous."

Lincoln scoffed. "We're not *that* messy, c'mon."

"Haven wanted that," Sophia said. The table went silent. She bristled nervously, glancing around. "I mean, the television thing. They wanted a camera crew, livestreamed prayer sessions, their own record label for worship music. All of it. That's when it was safe, believe it or not. Back in Texas. Saf*er*, I guess." The comment came out of the blue. *You're disruptive.* She tried to silence the voice, but it filled her skull, her own and someone else's. *Talking when no one wants to hear you. Blunt as a rock, girl. Dense as—* "Sorry," she blurted, and cleared her throat. "What's unique about this one?"

"You're allowed to talk about it." Lincoln met her eyes. He shrugged, sipping his beer.

"Doesn't surprise me," Tehlor said. She covered her mouth, speaking around half-chewed food. "But yeah, what makes us so weird, huh? Besides, like . . ." She gestured between herself and Colin. "Ancestrally speaking, we're enemies. And the whole"—she waved her fork between Bishop and Lincoln—"fucking their dead husband thing, but—"

"Jesus, Tehlor," Bishop seethed.

"*What?* We're all adults. Can we just, I don't know, can we get over it? Can we *be* over it? Lincoln's here, he's back, you're pissed, I get it. I'll rub your feet, I'll buy you a pizza, I'll do your laundry for a month." Next to her, sitting on the table nibbling carrots and chard, Gunnhild squeaked. "But I can't put him back in the wall—" She slid her attention to Lincoln. "I mean, I *could*—" Then back to Bishop. "But I won't."

"You two were married?" Sophia asked. She cocked her head, glancing between the brujo and the wolf-man.

Colin finished chewing and swallowed, flashing his hand. "It's complicated, Sophia. I said the same thing a little while ago—"

"Seriously?" Bishop exclaimed, spitting sarcasm. Their fork clattered on the plate. "Now *you*?"

At that, Lincoln shook with laughter, muffling the sound with his palm.

Laughter hiccupped in Juniper's mouth too. She giggled, clumsy and genuine, and Sophia laughed along, mostly at herself, at her heart for its sudden quickness, at her face for flaring hot again.

Juniper tapped her glass against Bishop's bottle. "To patience," she said, tempering the last bit of laughter. She reached, tapping the rest of their beverages. "And to family." She clanked her glass against Sophia's last. When their eyes met, Sophia thought the floor had fallen out from underneath her. *So this is what it's like,* she thought. *This is desire, this is infatuation, this is sin.* "And to reawakening."

Tehlor shouted, "Skål!" and everyone drank.

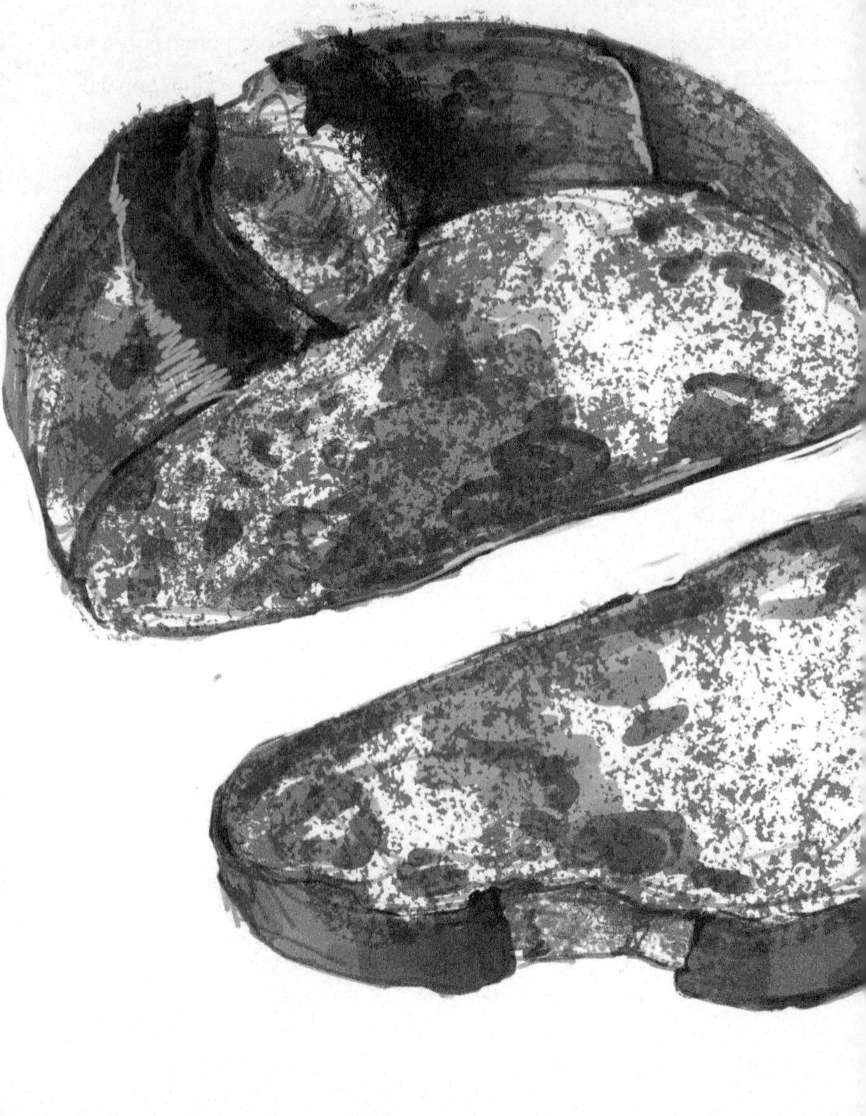

Chapter Six

The séance took place in the parlor.

Freshly blackened wicks burned atop virgin pillar candles clasped in fanciful holders. Juniper dunked two fingers into a small bowl and touched the water to her forehead, muttering a blessing under her breath. Bishop stood behind her, leaning against the seam where the wall met the domed window, and Tehlor arranged wide-mouthed mason jars in a line across the floor. While the psychic prepared, Tehlor unsheathed a crescent-shaped blade with a pearly handle and held out her palm.

Lincoln frowned, cradling Gunnhild under his chin. "Use me."

"I can bring her back—"

"Yeah, but still. Just use me."

Tehlor huffed out a laugh and relented, snatching his free wrist. "Use *us*," she corrected, and drove the blade into the heel of his palm. Lincoln winced but didn't make a sound. Tehlor hissed, gritting out a curse before she brought her hand—marred with a wound identical to his—to her face. Red streaked from her brows to the base of her throat.

Sophia couldn't make out Tehlor's whispered enchantment, but the witch's eyes frosted over, and the air thinned. Lincoln held his hand above her, allowing blood to splatter the bridge of her nose, drip over her lips, and darken her hairline. Cold washed through the house, scented like sea spray and ash.

Colin placed his hand on Sophia's shoulder and squeezed. "Don't be afraid," he said. "I've got you."

Do you? She swallowed uncomfortably, seated across from Juniper in an upholstered chair. The psychic slid the bowl to the far end of the round table and laid her arms flat, palms open. The medallion, etched with the image of her sacred saint, was paired with a garnet rosary. The crucifix dangling from the last bead was carved from obsidian, capturing candlelight like a firefly.

Sophia prayed. Nothing special. Nothing too desperate. But prayer all the same. She held scripture in her mind and thought of Galilee, a place of firsts and beginnings, where Christ might've walked, where ministry might've started.

Olive trees and chapped tongues. What a place it was, someone groaned, his voice low and rough, like the listing of a great ship. *Judea, though.* He hummed, as if pleased. *Home beckons, girl. Do you think it still bleeds? Is Akeldama still slick, still rotting?* The voice grew louder, deafening. *Call me prince of Gehenna; call me the one with a price—*

"Sophia," Juniper said, so urgently Sophia startled. She blinked. Time had slipped again. Around her, Colin, Tehlor, Lincoln, and Bishop stood at the ready, and Juniper stared, picking her apart. "You okay?"

Sophia nodded. "Did you . . ." She tilted her head back, glancing at Colin. "Did I say something?"

"Seemed a bit stuck is all," the priest said. His smile paled. "Go on, listen to June."

"Stuck," Juniper repeated. She transferred her gaze to Sophia. "More like entranced. Are we ready?"

"As ready as we'll ever be," Bishop said. They uncrossed their arms and gripped the back of Juniper's chair. Gold flooded their eyes and their pupils narrowed into diamonds. Their oversize shadow slinked across the floor on pawed feet, bent by candlelight.

Juniper inhaled deeply. "Let's begin, shall we? Mirror me. Place your arms above mine across the table."

Sophia did as she was told. Carefully, Juniper reached, securing her hands around Sophia's forearms. Sophia did the same, gripping Juniper beneath the dent of each elbow. She called for bravery. Rallied strength and swore to be fearless. She stole a glance at Tehlor. The witch stared back at her, and Sophia thought of Valkyrie, of everything Tehlor had become by the sheer will of her gods. *What will my God ever make of me?* She turned back toward Juniper and tried to ignore the soft press of the psychic's fingertips on her flesh. *What am I worth?*

"Join hands," Juniper said.

The four practitioners formed a circle around the table and clasped hands.

"See, priest, I'm not so bad," Lincoln cooed.

Juniper shushed the pair before Colin could respond. She met Sophia's gaze and stayed there. Her chest expanded on a long, steady breath.

"I am found wanting," Juniper said. Her voice lifted, stronger and louder than Sophia expected. The color in Juniper's eyes gleamed, replaced by molten gold. "Would spirit grant me an audience?"

Are you from Endor? The voice boomed in Sophia's skull. She winced, squeezing her eyes shut. *The road to Damascus is riddled with vermin. Weep, dead caller, for those with gifts burn brightest in perdition.*

"He's here," Sophia whispered.

"Who?" Juniper asked.

The candlelight blurred and stretched as Sophia fell backward, tumbling into herself. *No.* She fumbled, attempting to anchor to her skeleton. *Stop.* Tried to resist. *Don't.* But the rift yawned open, and she could do nothing except peer out from within, a passenger inside her own body. She lurched forward in the chair, gripping Juniper's arms harder. She saw flashes of her body reflected in the rosary around Juniper's neck. Watched herself become unrecognizable in the reflection on the curved window behind the table.

Black-eyed and horrific, pale and unknown, Sophia De'voreaux devolved into someone else entirely.

"Hemlock grew in Eden too," Sophia said, but the voice was not her own. It came from deep within, rumbling out of her gaping mouth. Her lips twitched. Her tongue, lifeless, began to dry. "Fruit fell and rotted. Corpses soured in the sun. Death had no name, but my future was sealed, nonetheless. My *destiny*," she spat, closing her lips around the word, snapping at it, "was a predetermined noose, sahira."

"Do you have a name, spirit?" Juniper asked.

"Do not take me for a fool," Sophia shouted. The voice boomed, howling, roaring, crashing, as if several animals had been stitched into one singular beast, mimicking an ocean, an earthquake. Other spirits clamored inside her, pushing against her skin, searching for a way out. She felt breakable. Yanked in one direction, then another. "And he said to me: I will tell you the mysteries of the kingdom, brother. But the ink of my gospel bled into the streets, transcribed for no one, spoken to no one, and the book was better for it."

"Judas Iscariot," Colin said. He muttered something else under his breath. A prayer of some sort. *Saint in the Armory, give strength to the downtrodden—*

"My name in your mouth!" Sophia's jaw stretched wider. She felt trapped in her body, drowning, tossed by unseen waves. "Filth," she hissed, snapping her teeth. Bone clanked. Her mouth rattled. Soreness bloomed in her gums. "What a sorry thing you are, searching for redemption in *me*."

Juniper dug her fingernails into Sophia's pale arms. "No one is exempt from redemption, spirit. Even you can be forgiven."

"I am king of the dead," she bellowed. Her jaw cracked. Sophia wanted to scream, wanted to claw her way out of her own body, wanted the séance to end. Pain became strange and distant, finding her like a ripple traveling outward. Only the smallest, shallowest bit made contact. The rest afflicted her apprehended body, piloted by incorporeal entities.

Possession was ugly. Familiar and brutal and miserable, like a collar buckled too tightly, like a hand on her nape, holding her down. Sophia thrashed inside herself. Hit and kicked and tried to reach for her teeth, for her fingernails, for tiny, organic weapons.

"Let me in, king," Juniper whispered. Her voice careened into the cavernous waste where Sophia writhed and shrieked.

Juniper was a fast-moving jungle, tendrils prodding every crevice, blooming bright and warm in the darkness. The lichen inside Sophia had a source. Sophia felt it growing, bursting, widening with every ghost who tried to sneak through time and find a new place to haunt. The controlling spirit—*Judas, Judas, Judas*—raged against Juniper's interference. His presence grew, deafening and oppressive, and Sophia could not hear, or move, or breathe. She saw herself—biting at the air, teeth cracking together, eyes like polished onyx—and wanted desperately to evacuate her own body. To place herself somewhere, anywhere else. Her spine locked. Laughter—maniacal, angry laughter—skidded out of her. Blood, the taste, the smell, became overwhelming. It stained the roof of her mouth, splattered the back of her throat, and poured from her nose.

"See," Amy said, tenderness foreign and sudden. She was a wraith, sliding through the split seam dividing life from death. "You were always meant for this, honey. One, two, we're comin' for you," she sang, sighing pleasantly. "Three, four . . ." Behind her sister's voice, Sophia heard shouting, hollering, breakage. She turned within herself, facing blackness, shadow—nothing, so much nothing. Two hands shot out, landing on each cheek, clutching hard. Amy's busted, eyeless face, gouged and broken, filled Sophia's vision. Tar-like liquid oozed between her teeth. Old blood crusted her nostrils. Her voice became an inhuman growl. "Burn the whore."

Sophia couldn't break away. She was caged in a body she'd once known, in her own temple. *Yes,* she thought, *burn me down.*

"Sophia," Juniper snapped. Her voice cut through the darkness.

Heretic, someone hissed. A scream lodged in Sophia's throat.

"Look at me," Juniper said.

Sophia cracked her eyes open. The suddenness of her was startling. Darkness pressed on the light haloing the psychic. Amy was gone, and Juniper stood in her place, golden, glowing. She breathed like she'd been running. Her aura flickered. *You look like Mary,* Sophia almost said. *Like Holy Mother.* But she sobbed instead.

The scream trapped inside her became a storm. Something she could wield. Something she could harness. But as she reached, tangling her fingers in the feeling, she couldn't find the strength to release it.

"Come back," Juniper said, nodding.

The pit where'd she'd fallen was like quicksand. Invisible hands latched around her ankles, tugged at her clothes, and cuffed her wrists. *This is the river Styx, this is Xibalba, this is the place before Hell.* Cries and chatter came and went, some familiar, some not. Judas spewed and gurgled, speaking a language she didn't know. Closer, Colin's voice ricocheted—*Michael, mighty and merciful, do not leave us stranded in our time of need*—and Tehlor called out—*Sophia! C'mon, get her back! What the fuck is happening, get her*—and Bishop's jaguar snarled close by. But it was Juniper who remained buried in her consciousness, holding tight to her spirit.

"They can't have you," she rasped. Desperation looked strange on her. She set her teeth and narrowed her eyes. "Come on, Sophia, come back. You have to decide, you have to make the choice—*wake up!*"

Gold, frankincense, myrrh, Sophia thought. *Wise men once looked to a planet masquerading as a star and found their way through the dark.*

"Wake up," Juniper shouted, thumbs situated at each corner of Sophia's mouth.

Move, priest. Lincoln. *Your angels aren't coming this time.*

"Please, Sophia." The psychic shook her head. "Follow me—"

The volume increased tenfold. Judas, Amy, Kimberly—all the spiritual residue leaking into her from purgatory—screamed at the very same time. Agony racked Sophia's small frame. Pain. Visceral, hellish *pain* shot through her chest, singed her throat, burned her bones. One moment, she was facing Juniper Castle, trapped in darkness, and the next, she was standing outside herself, watching Lincoln Stone press his bare hand to the base of her neck.

You're burning, someone said, wailing through her skull. *We're burning!*

Sophia surveyed the scene. Tehlor covered her mouth with both hands. Bishop turned away; their lips folded into a grimace. Colin, reaching for her, surrounded by silver light, and Juniper rising from her chair, mouth agape mid-shout. Lincoln's palm glowed red-hot.

Skin sizzled. *Her skin*. Again, time had slowed to a crawl, but the second Sophia leaned toward herself, she regained control.

Coming back felt like dying. It was the terrifying part. The hard part.

The first thing she did was gasp, filling her lungs until they hurt.

The second thing she did was scream. No sound came, though. Only the action, only the intention. She thrust both hands out, hitting Lincoln's wide chest, and jumped to her feet, sending the chair toppling over behind her. The delicate flesh between her collarbones sizzled, charred from Lincoln's hellfire. She reached for the wound but stopped, holding her trembling hands above the blackened palm print.

Everyone shouted her name. Tehlor darted toward her, Colin set his hand on her shoulder, Juniper said something sharp in Spanish, and Lincoln sighed. Bishop was the only one who kept their distance, watching her from the other side of the table.

"Unnecessary," Colin hissed at Lincoln.

"Right, because your *prayers* sure got the job done, exorcist," Lincoln snapped back.

"We'll fix you up," Tehlor said, hushed, nodding vigorously. "Bishop's a healer, they can—"

Sophia jerked away. She felt loose in her body. Clumsy, almost. Like she'd shrugged on a thrift store jacket or stepped into pants two sizes too big. Part of her wanted to fall to her knees. A larger, louder part of her, took shelter in the comfortable repetition of a childhood mantra, said *digger, listener, runner*. Before she could think better of it, Sophia ran. She elbowed her way past Lincoln and flew through the front door.

Colin rushed after her. "Wait!"

"Let her go," Juniper said. Her voice grew distant as Sophia's bare feet smacked the pavement. "I'll find her."

Night fell over West Hollywood, disrupted by neon bar signs and brightly lit food trucks. People dressed in designer clothes stomped on sidewalks and puffed vape pens outside of crowded clubs. Most of them didn't look at her, but a few did. Perfectly curled eyelashes flicked, following Sophia's jilted movements. Pouty lips moved quickly around commentary she couldn't hear spoken casually to people she didn't know. Someone glanced at her naked feet. Another person averted their gaze, shying away from the sight of her. When she focused, she noticed the uninvited. Graying skin, broken flesh, burial clothes. The dead mingled with the living, watching Sophia stumble along, the final girl in a cheap horror flick.

She still felt incompatible with her body, like a program downloaded into the wrong machine.

The busy city block gave way to lamplit neighborhoods and darkened alleys. She skirted along the edge of the populated areas, startling at the gruff sound of a nearby bark and the clatter of a metal trash can. People shouted, laughter echoed, and Sophia quickened her pace, bundling her sleeves into each sweaty palm. *Los Angeles isn't beautiful.* The thought came and went as she dodged a broken bottle. *None of this is beautiful.*

Not the escape, not the grief, not the magic.

"Lord, I come to you orphaned," she choked out, murmuring the prayer under her breath. "In need of a shepherd. For when Moses saw the burning bush, he knew it was you, and when the angel appeared to Abraham, he said *do not be afraid,* but I am afraid. I'm scared of dying, I'm scared of living, I'm scared of what I became at the revival and what I'm becoming now. I need you to show me." Her throat tightened. She turned down a quiet street and walked toward a warehouse covered in graffiti. "Show me, Almighty. Show me what I am. *Tell* me what I'm supposed to do."

God didn't answer.

Street art scrawled across the brick carcass at the end of the street. Garbage littered the ground next to discarded sleeping bags and a torn tent. Sophia avoided a brownish puddle and came to stand in front of a dusty window. A jagged crack split the glass down the middle. Beyond it, she saw the outline of a handmade half-pipe and the remnants of a broken skateboard.

"Prince of a thousand enemies." Amy De'voreaux's voice shattered the silence. She bent Sophia's reflection, apprehending familiarity, becoming false and lucid. "When they catch you, they'll kill you. That's how it goes, right?"

Amy was far truer than she'd ever been before. The open gash below her chin and the tunnel in her torso had ripened, crusted over with dried blood. Her eyes, gouged, still held life, somehow. They glinted, catlike and primal. Lifeless hair hung around her in matted locks and she bared her teeth, slick with grime and decay. Sophia looked at her for longer than she cared to. Longer than she ever had since the revival.

"Yeah, that's how it goes," Sophia said, sniffling. She scrubbed her hand beneath her nose. "Why are you still here? How are you—"

"Holy vessel, we made you, remember? And in this holding, we will emerge victorious and new." Amy's grin widened. Black dripped from the crack between her lips, slicing up one side of her face. Her voice deepened, warping. "The ultimate sacrifice will be made, and the lamb will know nothing of our kingdom on Earth. She'll *burn.*" Amy leaned closer. It was impossible, but Sophia watched her ghostly breath fog the glass. "And scream and sit with her sin for eternity. Are you ready, carrier of the betrayer? Are you ready for descension?"

Her mouth wobbled. Chest clenched. She wanted to reach through the glass and snag a lock of her sister's hair. Keep a bit of her. "Say something real." *Tell me you love me. Tell me you hate me. Tell me you forgive me.* "Please."

Amy's grin immediately fell. "Hutch rabbit," she hissed, laughter strangling each word. "Cunning and full of tricks."

"I'm sorry," Sophia said, because it might've been her only chance to say it.

"Sorry?" Amy lurched forward. Her hand shot out, hardly human, scaled with frostbite and chew marks from insects. She grappled for Sophia's neck. "Liar. You left me to rot in those woods, little girl. You left me for the animals. Defiler! Transgressor! The soldiers of the Lord will carve Christ's name into your stomach and your womb will rot, betrayer—"

"*You* betrayed *me*!" Sophia opened her mouth and a sound like a scream—sharper, worse—shot from her. She'd meant to shout, to yell, to cry, but power surged through her, evacuating in a shrill burst.

The window shattered. A streetlight down the block exploded, sinking the warehouse, Sophia, and anyone else nearby into thicker darkness. The spectral sound carried, shredding the air. Somewhere close, a car alarm blared. She stumbled backward and pawed at her throat, searching for the remnants of Amy's cold grip. Nothing. Her pinkie brushed the edge of the raw print from Lincoln's hand. She winced.

"You betrayed me, Amy," she said again, softer, hardly a whisper, and took another step away from the building. "But you're right, I'm not sorry." Her voice quaked. She shook her head. "I'm not fuckin' sorry, you hear me?" She pitched herself forward on her tiptoes and shouted, "I'm not sorry!"

Movement darted across the empty building. Sophia flinched at first, anticipating a ghoulish creature to sprint from the pitch. But it was light that came and went, streaking the brick in a smooth swoop. She didn't recognize the motorcycle at first, but as the bike rumbled, tires rolling closer, Sophia noticed the familiar matte-black paint and Juniper's strong legs straddling the seat.

Juniper cut the engine, lowered the kickstand, and ripped off her helmet. Her fishtail braid swung. She took off a small backpack and reached inside, tossing a pair of slip-on flats at Sophia's dirty feet.

"Good way to get tetanus," Juniper said.

Sophia swallowed the sting in her throat. "How'd you find me?"

The psychic brought her gloved hand to her mouth and bit the tip of her finger, working the black leather off with her teeth. Sophia watched, transfixed, and her pulse quickened. Once Juniper's hand was free, she reached into her pocket and dropped a crystal pendulum from her palm. The bauble dangled by its chain.

"You're a beacon. Easy to find." She tucked the pendulum back into her pocket and heaved a sigh. "You can't just run off like that, Sophia. This isn't Gideon. You could get—"

"Hurt?" Sophia laughed, bouncing in place as she yanked the right shoe on. "Abducted? Robbed? I just had a conversation with my dead sister, and I"—she waved at the warehouse—"exploded a window, and before that, I had *you* probing around in my head, and Judas Iscariot talking about . . ." She caught herself before she fell and growled, pulling the left ballerina flat into place. "... *destiny* and shit. Some night prowler copycat is the least of my worries right now, okay?"

Juniper tilted her head. Her charcoal jacket was tight and ribbed, matching sturdy boots and jet-black pants. She was a culmination of many things Sophia had avoided for most of her life. Free, capable, confident, sufficient. Self-made. Designed against submission. She narrowed her eyes, staring hard at Sophia's throat. Sophia took the opportunity to study her too. To fixate on Juniper's fine mouth and strong jaw, to imagine her flustered and unrefined.

"You exploded a window?"

Sophia bristled. "Yeah, I don't . . . I just . . . I screamed and it shattered."

"What kind of scream, Sophia?"

She shrugged helplessly. "I don't know, June. You're the expert."

Juniper unzipped her jacket and stripped it away, exposing a half-buttoned white top tucked into her pants. She tossed the jacket at Sophia, then held the backpack out to her.

Sophia fumbled to catch it. "What?"

"I can't wear the pack with you on the back. Put it on."

Sophia gave the motorcycle a quick scan. Really, she didn't have much of a choice. But the idea of it—being that close, being out of control—made her entire body constrict. She slipped her arms through the warm, buttery sleeves, scented like sandalwood and almond, and looped the backpack straps over her shoulders. Juniper invaded her senses. She cleared her throat, masking her nerves with a frown. Juniper shifted forward in the seat and handed Sophia the helmet.

Sophia furrowed her brow. "That's yours, I can't—"

"Take it."

Reluctantly, she took the helmet.

"Get on," Juniper said.

Sophia swung her leg over the seat and adjusted the chin strap on the helmet, pulling it tight. The proximity between her and Juniper was instantly eaten away.

Juniper glanced over her shoulder. "Hold on."

"What?"

"Hold on to me."

Something hot and new flared in Sophia's gut. She aligned herself against Juniper, legs spread, crotch pressed to her ass, and gripped her waist, setting her thumbs above jutting hip bone. The bike roared to life, humming beneath them, and when Juniper leaned forward, Sophia did too. Juniper gripped the handles and the bike sped forward. Sophia tightened her grip. Everything blurred after that. It was Juniper's jacket zipped to her chin, and the cool night air skimming her clothes, and Juniper's braid whipping against the helmet. It was residual power—uncertain and unknown—lingering in her core, and the dizzying rush of finality beating in her chest. *I'm going to die*, Sophia thought, and held on to Juniper tighter. *But please, God, not yet, not yet.*

Red brake lights streamed by in Sophia's peripheral as Juniper weaved through the city. The bike accelerated, faster, *faster*. Sophia kept her eyes open, watching the world soften and melt, palm trees running into skyscrapers, merging like watercolors. They cruised a windy road toward Griffith Observatory and stopped at a lookout near the Hollywood Sign. Juniper cut the engine again and waited for Sophia to dismount before she swung her leg over the seat and stood.

The Hollywood hills were ripe with desert beauty. Cacti sprouted between busheled buckwheat. Crisp bramble and honeysuckle hugged the trail and sycamores speared the skyline. The moon hung high above the city, tinted orange and blanketed by smog.

Sophia set the helmet on the seat and swiped her hand through her hair. When she tried to take off the jacket, Juniper tugged the lapels, securing the garment.

"Looks good on you," Juniper said. She placed a bent knuckle beneath Sophia's chin and shifted her attention to the mark on her neck. "Bishop's making a salve." She sighed. Her breath coasted the sensitive, pink wound. Sophia shivered. Cursed God. Thanked God. "That scream," she tested, lifting a brow. "Think you could do it again?"

"Why?" Sophia asked, a little out of breath, a little dazed.

"Because when you spend enough time in the presence of death, sometimes you come across the opportunity to form an outside relationship with it. Rare, obviously. But you're in the rarest circumstance I can imagine."

"An outside relationship . . . ?"

"Power is a fickle thing."

Sophia shook her head. "I don't have power—I've never had power."

The psychic gave a short, breathy laugh, and Sophia felt it everywhere.

"What set you off?" Juniper asked.

Sophia's head spun. "What?"

"What did it? What set you off?" Juniper stepped closer, craned over her.

"Nothing—I got scared, I—"

"You got pissed."

"Back up," Sophia snapped, shying away. Her heart pounded. Vision doubled. Panic twisted behind her ribs.

Juniper snatched her wrist. "C'mon, what did it? Show me—"

Sophia ripped away. Her voice lifted, electric and haunting, and burst from her. "I said *back off*!"

A murder of sleepy crows honked and cawed, fleeing from a valley oak. That same icy sound sent Juniper's braid twirling behind her. It rippled her shirt. Caused the bike to creak on its kickstand. Sophia heaved in a shaky breath and met Juniper's sharp, curious gaze. The psychic made a confident noise, *ah,* like she'd aced a quiz. She brushed her gloved fingers over Sophia's knuckles, an apology written in touch.

"See," Juniper cooed. "An unbecoming can lead to something else, no?"

Sophia shook her head. "First I'm dying, now I'm—"

"Still dying."

"Great."

"A banshee isn't born," she said, and walked toward the overlook. "She's made."

Banshee. Sophia flexed her toes, hands, legs, and recognized the effortless quiet encapsulating her mind. Ever since her explosion at the warehouse, the dead had gone silent. She trailed after Juniper, repeating the term to herself, *banshee,* and relived moments ago, gripping Juniper's waist, racing through the city. *I want to go back.* She stood at the edge of the trail, counting glittering headlights instead of stars. *I want to stay with you, like that.*

"Removing the Breath of Judas will save your life, but it won't undo the damage here." She tapped her sternum, gesturing to her heart, then tapped her temple. "Or here. You understand that, right?"

Sophia curled her bandaged hand into a fist. Pain pulsed in the puncture on her palm. *Yeah, I know.* She stayed silent, though, spinning through the aftermath of *power* and *banshee* and *dying* and *life.*

Juniper looked out over the city too. "Everything evolves. You're being spiritually attacked, so your spirit's figuring out how to protect itself. Desperate times, desperate measures. Do you know what I mean when I say banshee?"

No. She shook her head. *Sort of.*

"A woman who makes death's presence known."

"Like Eve?" Sophia held her breath until her chest ached.

Juniper cocked her head.

"Before the serpent entered Eden, we knew nothing of sin. Nothing of death, or consequence, or mortality. Eve made death's presence known," Sophia said. She blinked at the horizon before turning to look at Juniper, fist still clenched, heart still hammering. "Our mother, defiler." The last three syllables scraped her throat, stolen from Amy's ghost.

"Maybe. But imagine being Adam, waking one morning to a bloody gash and a missing bone, remade to perfection," Juniper said. "Father of all, defiled."

Sophia pulled the jacket tighter around her. It was much too big, falling comfortably around her shoulders. "So, what, I can super-scream?"

Juniper laughed in her throat. "In time, you'll probably track death from one place to the next. Sense patterns in cursed bloodlines, tap into the afterlife, communicate with spirits—"

"I don't want *any* of that, like, none of it, I—"

"Evolution isn't negotiable."

She opened her mouth to argue, then pulled it shut. *God, do you hear me? Are you listening?* She met Juniper's eyes. "Can you teach me?"

"Maybe. First, I need to exorcise the Breath of Judas and put it somewhere else. It won't be simple, I'm afraid. But I might have an idea."

"I'm listening."

"I don't like it. Colin *really* won't like it."

"I'm not Colin," Sophia bit out. She exhaled sharply through her nose. "Tell me."

"Judas is siphoning your life force to keep himself rooted inside you. That gateway, whatever fissure the Breath of Judas opened, is alive because it's attached to a living vessel. Like I said, you're haunted. But houses don't have heartbeats." Her mouth tightened. "The relic was planted in you during a death ritual, right?" When Sophia nodded, Juniper clucked her tongue. "Then I think you know where I'm going with this."

Sophia's jaw slackened. "You want to . . . To kill me . . . ? You think—that's your plan?" She sputtered out a laugh. Her eyes stung. "*Kill me* is the plan?"

"I said I didn't like it," she said matter-of-factly.

"Yeah, no shit."

"If you leave your body like you did tonight, I can extract the Breath of Judas. But we need another vessel for the relic and you need a tether."

"A tether?"

"Something to keep you here," she clarified. "Faith, to be frank."

"I have faith."

"You have OCD," Juniper deadpanned, too playful to be serious, too serious to be taken lightly. She flashed a grin and winked. "I'm kidding. But you will need a god or a saint—something to focus on, someone to count on."

Sophia swallowed hard. "And you'll bring me back?"

"I'll bring you back," Juniper said, nodding. "I know it's scary, but being what you are, doing what you've done. There's no shame in that."

"What, being a vessel, being a banshee?"

"Surviving."

"Oh no, there's shame in my survival," she assured, huffing out a laugh. She remembered the way Kimberly's fingernails brought back bits of her sister. How blood stained the snow. "Trust me."

Juniper was quiet for a moment. Almost too long. "There's strength in you. El oído wouldn't manifest if you didn't deserve it. Seeing beyond what we're given is a beautiful thing and someone out there, someone greater than us saw you."

"Yeah, what about you," Sophia braved. "Do you *see me*, Castle? Do you think I'm beautiful?"

Juniper's lips curved. "I think you're tempting."

"Eve and the apple," Sophia said. The original mother. Seeker. Destroyer. "Careful."

"Do you think Genesis was really about the fruit? I always thought it was about the snake." Juniper tapped Sophia's chin with her gloved thumb. Leather filled her nostrils. She almost opened her mouth, almost snagged Juniper's hand with her teeth. "Everyone blames Eve, yet we thank God for a world the devil offered her."

Sophia swallowed hard. "A world we weren't supposed to have."

"Says who?" she dared.

The question was rhetorical, but Sophia still struggled with an answer. God, Christ, Almighty, Creator. She thought of Noah, and the Book of Enoch, and the plagues that ravaged Egypt. Everything her righteous, punishing God had done once Eden became a past life.

If he could not keep it from her, he would destroy it to spite her, a ghost said. Judas, maybe.

"You'll bring me back," Sophia said again, standing beside the bike.

Juniper adjusted the strap on the helmet, fastening it beneath Sophia's chin. "I'll bring you back."

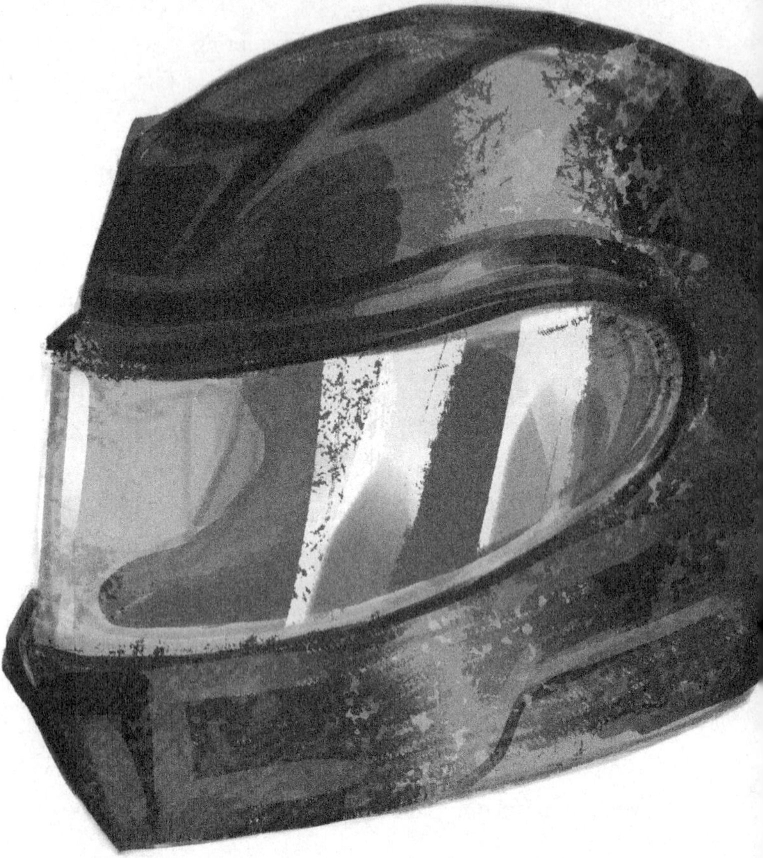

Chapter Seven

The Belle House glowed in the witching hour. Sophia hadn't expected anyone to be awake, but when Juniper propped the door with her foot, the pair were greeted by Colin, Bishop, Lincoln, and Tehlor seated around the parlor table, talking quietly between sips from steaming mugs. Gunnhild turned toward Sophia from her perch on Tehlor's shoulder and stretched out her snout. Sophia scratched the rat's fuzzy head, focusing on the animal rather than the people.

"Sorry, kid," Lincoln said. Sincerity sounded strange in his mouth. Misplaced. He wiggled his nose and flattened his wolfish ears. "We couldn't get you back. Ran out of options."

"Bishop's medicinal balms are very good, trust me," Colin assured.

Sophia shifted her gaze to Bishop. The brujo looked back at her over the black rim of their glasses and twisted their wrist, grinding an aloe leaf with a stone pestle. They stood and shrugged toward the kitchen.

Juniper placed her palm on the small of Sophia's back and gave a small, encouraging push. "Go on. Fix some tea while you're in there."

Truthfully, she craved a hot shower. Desperately wanted to scrub away the séance and let the unfamiliar self-defense—*magic*—her spirit had embraced run down the drain. But Bishop inclined their head as they walked past, disappearing through the beaded curtain, and Sophia knew following them was her only option. *Appease the group, make a plan, go to bed.* Beads rolled across her shoulder. The dimly lit kitchen, spotless despite the mess they'd made fixing dinner, still smelled like dark chocolate and spiced meat. She leaned against the island next to Bishop, waiting for instruction.

Bishop shot her a patient look. "I hated Lincoln," they whispered, nodding as if to convince themself. "Still do, I guess . . ." They gathered a glob of the greenish paste and gestured to her neck. "But for once, he's not lying. I couldn't get you back, Colin couldn't, Tehlor couldn't—"

"Pain is the ultimate equalizer," Sophia said, and lifted her chin. "It did the job."

They arched a brow. "True. But I don't think he *wanted* to hurt you." They smeared salve over the burn. She flinched, bracing for discomfort. The balm had the texture of cold pudding. "That's all."

"Did he want to hurt you?"

Bishop's mouth thinned. "Good question. Here, in this moment, yeah, I think he did. Ask me again in six months and my answer might be different."

"Hurt has a shelf life, huh?" She closed her eyes, savoring the tingly relief coursing through the pinkened handprint.

"I killed him the first time around." They met her gaze, watching her carefully. "Neither one of us will ask for forgiveness, and neither one of us will give it, but yeah, I think hurt has a shelf life. Sometimes it has to."

"What's in this stuff?"

"Herbs, aloe, milk, magic."

Magic. The concept still shook her. "Do you trust her?"

Bishop met her eyes. "Tehlor? Depends on the day."

"Juniper."

They chewed their cheek and leaned forward, whispering an incantation against sore skin. Spanish fluttered from them, quick-tongued and raspy, until they rounded their lips and exhaled. Magic, power, sacrifice—a trio of uncanniness she couldn't parse. She didn't know if they were cousins or enemies, if magic came from power, if sacrifice was the cause or effect of either or both, but she closed her eyes and allowed Bishop's warmth to pass through the burn and sink into her body. As her flesh knitted together, she chased their ethereal strength and heard the mindful click of their tongue. She cracked her eyes open, met with gold flaring outward from their pupils.

"I learn lessons the hard way." They placed their finger on her jaw, pushing left, then right. "And after my last one, I swore off trusting anyone for a while. Colin fucked that up," they mumbled, smiling sheepishly. They nodded, pleased with their work, and dropped their hand. "But if I were you, I'd trust her."

"If *you* were *me*? That's a real ass-backward way to say *no*," she said.

At that, Bishop laughed. It came from their belly, strong and surprising. "Fine, I'll rephrase. If I were you, I wouldn't trust anyone. Which you don't—I can tell. But if you were *going* to trust anyone, I'd let it be her."

"And your priest," she said.

Bishop's smile split into a grin. "And my priest."

Tehlor's delighted voice shook the house, flitting from the adjoining room. "You're a banshee now, huh?"

Bishop lifted an eyebrow. The metallic flash dancing behind their lashes flickered out. *Banshee,* they mouthed, silently asking for clarification. Sophia shrugged and gave a curt nod. *I don't know,* she wanted to say. Vessel, banshee, betrayer, defiler. She'd been called a lot of things recently, but before that, she'd always been Sophia. Pretty, but not as beautiful as her sister, and holy, but not as clean as she could be, and obedient, but not as submissive as she should've been. She'd kissed boys after choir and snuck glances at girls in the locker room. Said *yes ma'am* and *no sir* and *please* and *thank you*. Offered blessings to newcomers who wandered into Haven. Prayed like someone listened. Flinched at the sound of too-bright lights and held food in her mouth for years before swallowing. Banshee was new, but she'd always been something to someone. Fixable, controllable, irredeemable.

"Thank you," she said to Bishop, and cleared her throat, stepping through the curtain. "I'm dying," she corrected, trailing her hand along the back of the sofa. "Proximity to death made me somethin' new, I guess."

Colin inclined his head. "Some*one* made you new."

Sophia stiffened. His statement needled her.

"It's late," Lincoln said. He drained the rest of his beverage and lolled his head, granting Sophia a once-over. "You look tired."

"Let's rest, then." Relief rang heavy in Juniper's voice. "We'll make a plan in the morning."

When Tehlor turned toward Sophia, her rat did too. Gunnhild blinked. The witch blinked. They breathed at once. "Get some sleep, okay?"

Sophia nodded. She flicked her attention to Lincoln and tipped her chin. Her smile was stony and fraught, but he smiled back and there was forgiveness in that, somehow. *You did what you had to* written in the quiet pass of two people suspended postmortem. He might've been the only one who understood that part of her. The shared experience of dying and returning. Coming back wrong.

As Sophia made for the stairs, Colin touched her shoulder. "Bishop mended you?"

"They did, yeah," she said.

He smiled faintly. "I . . . I'm sorry. For earlier, the séance," he said, clipped. "I meant to protect you—I *tried* to protect you. I hope you know that."

"I do." And it was the truth. Even in the dark, faced with her sister's corpse, she'd heard him calling for her. She'd heard them all. "You don't need to apologize."

Colin opened his mouth, but before he could continue, Bishop appeared beside him.

"C'mon, Colin. It's been a long night," they said, guiding him up the staircase. They shot Sophia an apologetic glance. "Good night."

"Thank you for . . ." She gestured loosely to her neck.

Bishop nodded over their shoulder, hand clutched in Colin's palm, and said, "Anytime."

Sophia waited for Colin and Bishop to reach the landing before she followed.

Juniper cleared her throat from the foyer. "Good night, Sophia."

She paused near the top of the staircase and turned, scanning Juniper. Her wild braid, almost entirely unwoven by the wind, hung over her shoulder, and the top of her crisp, pale shirt was unbuttoned, framing the bold lettering on a Calvin Klein bralette. Like that, dark eyeliner smudged around her lashes, thumbs tucked into her belt loops, expression earnest and true, Juniper Castle became a terrifying, thrilling thing. *Conquest.* The word rang in Sophia's mind, uttered from a ghost.

"See you in the morning," Sophia said.

Juniper nodded. "Dream peacefully."

"You too."

She wanted to say a thousand things. Wanted to ask a thousand questions. *What's so tempting about me? Thank you for bringing me back. Are you lonely? You have beautiful everything. Do the dead tell you about me? I'll be your banshee if it's what you want. Did my hands on your waist make you blush? I'm still warm from it, from you.* But Sophia climbed the stairs instead.

She left her clothes piled on the bathroom floor and braced against the shower wall, watching suds circle the drain between her feet. Her spine lengthened. Chatter whispered in her left temple, flickering like a dying bulb. *Reaper, free the displaced.* She closed her eyes. The water was almost too hot to bear. The steam almost too thick. *Let us out.*

After she'd scrubbed her hair and pressed a washcloth to her tender neck, she twisted the knob and stepped onto the fuzzy rug, staring at her distorted reflection. Steam pulled her this way and that. She was an oddity on the glass, faceless and unrecognizable.

"You can't have me," she whispered. To Judas, to Amy, to Kimberly, to every ghost pushing at the seams of her soul. She spoke to the rift, too, to the place inside her making false promises to the dead. Water dripped from the faucet. She pulled a towel around herself and reached for the switch, killing the light with a quick flick.

A feminine purr rolled through the air, sending a shiver down Sophia's spine. It did not come from within, but instead, manifested from the darkness. Gently, like a feather, two words landed on the shell of her ear.

"You're mine."

Sophia dreamed of candlelight. How gold settled on the bridge of Juniper's nose and deepened the grooves around her upturned eyes. She chased the free fall after waking, snatching at leather and body heat. Her skin felt too tight, drawn close to her organs, squeezing relentlessly, and her heart revved as she blinked at the ceiling, stumbling out of a fading dreamscape.

Juniper, overlooking the city. Juniper, staring up at her from the foyer. Juniper, saying *amen*.

She swallowed to wet her throat and turned toward the balcony. Outside, the blue hour crept over Los Angeles, hardly illuminating the gauzy curtains. Birds chirped and early-morning traffic shushed through the neighborhood. Rain streaked the glass. A storm had come and gone sometime after she'd fallen asleep—after an unfamiliar voice, ghost, *presence* materialized from a thatch of shadows. *You're mine.* Feminine, terrifying. *You're mine.* Possessive, inhuman. Sophia had gone to sleep transfixed on the possibility of that voice.

It hadn't bloomed in her skull. Hadn't haunted her like the rest of them.

She remembered Colin's comment last night. *Someone made you new.* Remembered wailing at the warehouse. Remembered praying for a sign.

The floor wheezed beneath her bare feet. She dressed in corduroy pants and a hand-me-down turtleneck still scented like Tehlor's perfume and centered the crucifix between her collarbones. She crossed the hall and brushed her teeth in the bathroom. Kept her eyes on the sink. Blood splattered porcelain. Foam, saliva, gore.

Morning settled tenderly in the Belle House, rousing it from slumber like a doting mother. Sleepy whispers snuck through the gaps underneath closed doors. Cool, bluish tones poured through the stained window and striped the floor in the foyer. Song filled the kitchen accompanied by squeaky pantry hinges and a kettle on the cusp of whistling.

Sophia found Juniper there, teacup in hand, dressed in pastel nightclothes, humming a hymnal.

"Buenos días, conejita," Juniper said.

Sophia smirked. "Buenos días," she parroted, glancing over an array of ingredients neatly arranged on the kitchen island. "What're we cooking?"

"Apple turnovers." She tipped her cup toward the island. "If you're okay with that."

She rolled up her sleeves. "I'll need a knife."

Dawn was a baker's blessing. The sun barely broke over the horizon while Sophia peeled and sliced, sweetened and seasoned. Flour chalked the bandage around her palm and lemon juice perfumed the air. She vowed not to shrink as she spread egg wash over the pastry dough, hyperaware of Juniper's unwavering attention.

"You're like a hawk," Sophia mumbled.

Juniper tsked. "Not an owl?"

"Haven't heard you hoot," she teased.

She laughed and Sophia wanted to steal the sound. Wanted Juniper to pass that noise to her like smoke from a shared joint, exhaled, inhaled.

"I intended to make *you* breakfast. Can I help, at least?"

"Baking is my . . ." She shrugged, searching for the right word. "Solace, I guess. We need to cook down the apples before we bake 'em," Sophia said.

"I'm sure I can handle that." Juniper tightened her ponytail and took the sliced apples to the stove, upending the bowl into a pan. She added a dollop of butter, some vanilla syrup, and stirred in halved anise.

The kitchen smelled sweet and cozy, and Sophia appreciated the normalcy. She imagined what the shopfront of her own bakery might look like and decided to speak it into existence. "I'd have, like, those cute wooden racks," she said, and cleared her throat. "In my own place, I mean. My own bakery." When Juniper nodded, she kept going, apprehended by *maybe*, smitten by *one day*. "I think I'd go with the dark, desert theme. Lots of natural texture, potted cactus, neon signage, starry-patterned parchment paper, minimalist business cards . . ." She thought of focaccia, and Danish cheese, and gluten-free cupcakes. "I know it's kitschy—"

"It's not." Juniper shook her head. "Don't make light of your desires. If that's what you want, that's what you should get."

Sophia laughed under her breath, mostly at herself. "Sorry, I do that sometimes. Just . . . Just *talk*."

"I don't mind listening. Have you ever made pan dulce?"

She shook her head. "I've seen conchas before."

"I'll teach you."

"If I live," Sophia said.

Apples sizzled in the pan. Footsteps padded the second floor. She scolded herself for ruining the slow morning, still dewy and new, but every thought emptied the moment Juniper set her hands on either side of Sophia's hips and rested her chin on the slope of Sophia's shoulder.

"Well, if you die, haunt me," she said, so simply, before stepping away and opening the fridge.

What a morbid thing, how those last two words weakened Sophia's knees.

Your heart is monstrous, someone keened, crowing from the confines of her mind. *Full of teeth, awaiting a sword.*

"Comforting," Sophia joked, ignoring how her groin clenched, how her head spun.

Sophia finished the pastries and slid them into the oven while Lincoln sauntered through the beaded curtain followed by Tehlor, still dressed in pajamas, holding her rat in one hand and pawing at her eyes with the other. It wasn't long before Colin and Bishop joined them in the kitchen too.

"Whatchya makin'," Tehlor murmured.

"Turnovers," Juniper said. "Tea or coffee?"

To Lincoln's dismay, everyone else agreed on tea, so he conceded.

"Did you sleep all right?" Colin asked. He laid his hand on Sophia's arm as he reached for the honey in the pantry.

Sophia stood at the sink, rinsing sticky fruit juice and sugar from her hands. "I slept," she said, shrugging. "You?"

He mimicked her, lifting one shoulder. "Three hours, give or take."

"So the whole séance shindig was a hot mess," Tehlor said.

Bishop nodded, seated on the countertop, heels tapping a closed drawer. "And Sophia being a walking, talking portal to purgatory gave her the power of a dead caller."

"*But* that power isn't significant enough to salvage her life," Lincoln added.

Salvage. Sophia tasted the word like a penny on her tongue.

Juniper cleared her throat. "All true. I found the access point, though. Every corpse Sophia has directly or indirectly possessed is an active way station. My initial assessment was correct—the magic she used at the revival spreads like fungus. Which means the spiritual warfare won't stop until we contain the Breath of Judas." She tapped one fingernail against her teacup, *click, click, click.* "Since I doubt we could close the rift, I think we should extract it."

Tehlor laughed into her mug. "We're back at square one."

Juniper shot her a silencing glare. "I have an idea."

"Is it a good one?" The witch narrowed her eyes, meeting Juniper's glare with twice the venom.

"It's one that'll work."

"Down, girl," Lincoln teased, tugging Tehlor into his lap. He curled one arm around her, tightening like a leash, and lifted his mug with the other. "We're listening."

Juniper snorted. "If the Breath of Judas was bound to Sophia's body during a death ritual, then we can likely unbind it from her using the same formula." She shifted her attention from Tehlor to Colin. "You're familiar, no?"

"Bishop extracted stolen magic from inside a possessed corpse. That's a lot different than extracting dead magic from a living person," Colin said.

"Yes, but the transference wouldn't happen on this plane," Juniper said. She sipped her tea.

The oven beeped. Sophia slid on a mitt and retrieved the sticky turnovers.

"You want to kill her," Lincoln deadpanned.

Juniper nodded. "Momentarily."

"June," Colin warned, cinching his brow. "That's *extremely* dangerous."

"Sophia has a foothold," Juniper said, and gestured to Tehlor. "Like I said, every corpse she's directly or indirectly possessed is a way station. If Sophia can tap into Tehlor during the ritual, she'll have a living tether to this plane." She arched a thick, perfectly sculpted brow. "If you're strong enough to keep her steady, witch."

Tehlor's mouth tightened. "Careful, palm reader."

"She's strong enough," Lincoln said.

"How is Tehlor a living tether?" Bishop asked, bewildered.

Sophia sighed through her nose. "Because she almost died," she said, rolling the rest around in her mouth before shaping each word. "And I kept her here."

Bishop shot Tehlor a wild-eyed look. They pressed their lips together and exhaled sharply through their nose. Misfired worry shot through them like an arrow, and Sophia watched Bishop right themself against it. Strange, how they tempered concern to comfort their pride. She transferred the turnovers to a clean plate and took one for herself.

Colin hummed. "No wonder you developed a banshee's scream. Sounds like you've been dabbling in dead calling for a while now."

Sophia shrugged. She remembered Lincoln's bloody maw. How he snapped his teeth. *I've seen what you can do—bring her back!* "I didn't have a choice."

"Okay, so, Sophia uses Tehlor as a tether in the afterlife, somehow, then Juniper extracts the Breath of Judas and puts it where, exactly?" Bishop asked.

Juniper snorted. She slid her gaze to Colin. "You haven't used that box my brother gave you yet, have you?"

The exorcist quirked his head. Something fiery and bold sparked behind his eyes. "It just so happens, I haven't."

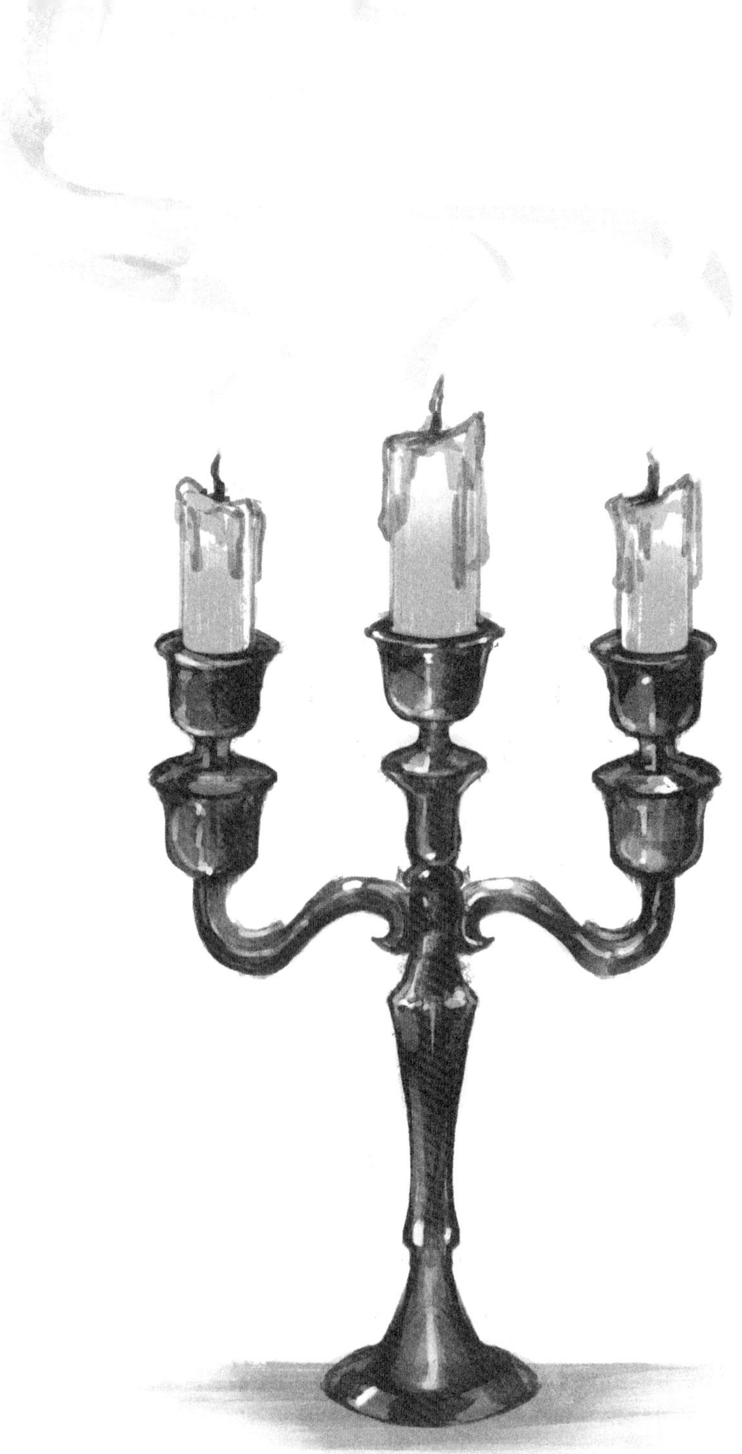

Chapter Eight

Botánica la Luz lived on a forgotten corner two blocks down from Venice Beach. Juniper parked in a crowded lot behind the building, lowering her kickstand while Sophia toed at the cement.

Sophia peeled off her helmet and turned toward the ocean, inhaling brine and salt. Soreness bloomed in her thighs, unused to gripping the small seat on Juniper's Triumph, but everything else, every*where* else felt electric. After breakfast, Tehlor and Lincoln volunteered to ready the Belle House for the extraction ritual and Bishop and Colin gathered Holy Water from the Los Angeles Cathedral. Juniper needed supplies, so Sophia accompanied her to the botánica. Hand-painted flowers brightened the white paint, curling over old brick, reaching toward the roof. Juniper shrugged off her jacket and draped it over her arm. Sophia did the same.

"Not as pretty as it is famous," Juniper said, gazing at the distant sea.

Sophia shook her head. "Plenty pretty for me."

"C'mon." She nudged Sophia with her elbow. "You ever been to a botánica before?"

"I've seen 'em. They're all over Austin."

Juniper held the canary-yellow door and waved Sophia inside.

Much was her initial thought. *Grand* came next. Then *bold* and *crowded* and *timely*.

Sturdy shelves filled with altar figurines, novena candles, and fragrant oil spanned each wall, surrounded by waist-high tables stocked with pamphlets, paperbacks, and salt satchels. Incense and shampoo, body lotion and room sprays. The botánica was a market steeped in magic yet rooted in familiar iconography. Sophia plucked a candle shaped like the Virgin Mary from a shelf and ran her thumb along Holy Mother's face. Someone at the counter spoke fast-lipped Spanish, asking question after question until they were satisfied. When they left, Sophia noticed a dark splotch soaking through the bottom of their paper bag.

The clerk wiped the counter with a rag. She greeted her and Juniper, offering a polite "Bienvenidos."

Juniper nodded. "Buenas tardes."

"What do you need?" Sophia asked.

"Florida Water, Quita Maldición, mandrake oil, candles." She shrugged and grabbed a plastic bag filled with leafy stems. The label read *Espanta Muerto Plant.* Her long fingers dusted pillar candles and incense cones. She paused over a figure of a skeletal saint much like the one beneath the staircase and uttered a prayer under her breath.

Sophia cocked her head. "Who is she?"

"Santa Muerte, saint of holy death, guardian of the displaced. She's my deity, I'm sure you've noticed."

"You pray to her?"

"I do," Juniper said. "She may not be God, but she's protected me far more than the almighty ever has. Do you have a saint?"

Joan, someone said. The same voice that'd crept from the shadows—cloaked in power, lilting and beautiful—coasted the shell of her ear. Sophia startled, dodging an invisible force. She swatted at nothing. Straightened in place and glanced over her shoulder, offering an apologetic smile to the ruffled clerk.

Juniper eyed her carefully. "Spirits?"

"No," she bit out, glancing around. "Something bigger. It's fine, it's gone. Sorry."

"Bigger?"

"Different."

"Different," Juniper repeated, nodding. She nudged her chin toward a display of rosaries strung from fake branches on a makeshift jewelry tree. "Pick one."

"Oh, I don't have any—"

"Pick one," Juniper insisted. She tipped her head as if to say *don't argue* and stepped around the table, gliding her pointer finger across hand-carved candles.

Sophia tested the weight of a few beads. Polished rose quartz cooled her skin, volcanic rock snagged the bandage around her palm, and her thumb glided over smooth glass. Two members of the Haven congregation had prayed with rosaries, counting each bead as they said their Act of Contrition or Hail Mary. But whenever Sophia had looked to relics, she'd always found herself snared by the book of Thomas. *I am all. Split a piece of wood and I am there. Lift a stone and you will find me* . She'd never needed a tool or a temple, but she gripped a small silver rosary with pearly beads anyway, sighing at the pleasant texture. She pressed her thumb to a saint's icon etched into flattened metal. Sword, helmet, armor.

"Joan of Arc." Juniper peeked over her shoulder and hummed, pleased. "Saint of liberation, strength, and rebellion. Good choice."

Sophia almost dropped the rosary. The hair on her nape stood. *Joan.* She replayed the strange, disembodied voice and clutched the beads tighter. Last night, it'd claimed her, *you're mine*, and right then, it guided her to an inevitable choice.

Who are you? She beamed the question outward. Countless voices chittered in her mind, whispering through the doorway to purgatory. Their answers overlapped, but one came forth, more familiar than the rest.

Mistaken daughter, Judas spat. *If only Hell could cage you.*

"Sophia?"

She blinked, snapping her attention to Juniper. Iron filled her mouth and she choked, cupping her hands beneath her chin before warm blood poured from both nostrils. She tried to say *sorry* but couldn't speak. Blood slickened the prayer beads and splattered on the saint's emblem. Warm, vibrant red slipped through her fingers and spilled on the linoleum.

"It's okay, you're all right," Juniper cooed. She set her hand between Sophia's shoulders and called for the clerk.

Sophia's vision tunneled. She swallowed and almost gagged. *He was a fighting animal,* she chanted, passages easing through her like an old friend, *fierce as a rat or a dog.* Juniper said her name again and pressed a damp cloth to her face. *He fought because he felt safer fighting.* Sophia coughed. Swallowed. Blinked rapidly. *He was brave, all right.* Finally, the blood stopped, and her heartbeat slowed, and Judas went quiet. *But it wasn't natural. That's why it was bound to finish him in the end.* She stared at the bloodied rosary nestled in her cupped palms and turned toward the raven-haired clerk. "I didn't mean to," she said, swallowing pasty carnage. "I'm sorry."

The wrinkled clerk turned to Juniper, flicking her eyes from the psychic's boots to her sequined violet top. "Demon?"

"Not quite," Juniper said. "Espíritu, doña."

The shopkeeper made a knowing noise and waved them toward the counter. "Yes," she said, pointing at Sophia's rosary. "Good protection." She spoke to Juniper in Spanish, repeating things when Juniper apologetically noted her quickness, and set a sheer baggie filled with stones on the counter. "In the bath with the salt," she said, pointing at Sophia. "No red meat. Try fish," she said, nodding curtly. "Fish is good. Oranges too." She stared at Juniper. "You have tangerine wash, yes?"

"Sí, doña," Juniper said.

"Wash the tub first. Then stones and salt, okay?"

"Muchas gracias."

"Sí, sí." She looked at Sophia. "Español?"

Sophia shook her head. She concentrated on her expression, softening her face, relaxing her mouth.

"Energy is alive. You can create it, can't destroy it," the clerk said. She nodded like Sophia understood, then continued. "Shoo away the bad and manifest the good, yes?"

"Yeah," Sophia said, clearing her throat. She wiped her nose with the cloth and tried to clean her new rosary, rolling the beads between the bloody fabric. "Thank you."

"No problem, mija. Be blessed."

Juniper paid for the supplies, thanked the clerk again, and steered Sophia toward the door. Sophia didn't realize she was still holding the towel until they were standing beside Juniper's bike. Sunlight brightened the crimson splotches darkening white cloth and caught the tiny chain-link on her rosary. She carefully rubbed another red streak away.

"I'll wash this and bring it back," Sophia mumbled, staring at the rag.

Juniper tsked. "I'm sure she doesn't expect it back, conejita."

That word again. Conejita. She swallowed the remaining trickle of blood and exhaled shakily. "I'll pay you back for all this, by the way. Them too. Colin, Bishop, Tehlor—"

"No one expects anything—"

"I will, though. I'll make it right, I'll—"

"Sophia—"

"I will," she bit out. She aimed the unrealistic frustration inward, but it was barbed. Spiny, like an urchin. Juniper raised her hand away from Sophia's back as if she'd been punctured. "No, don't . . ." She closed her eyes, breathing deeply, excavating her anger until it revealed itself as fear. Sometimes the truth was hard to parse inside emotions that were too big for her to carry. "I don't want to be a burden. I already *feel* like a problem you can't solve. Just let me say it, okay? Let me have that."

"Okay," she said, far gentler than Sophia expected. "You won't argue if I buy you lunch, though."

Sophia scrubbed the cloth beneath her nose and strung the rosary around her wrist. Joan of Arc's medallion tapped her palm, dangling above her bandaged stigmata.

"*Why?* Why help me?" Sophia asked. The question singed her tongue. "Am I a project? Is this some . . . some kind of test of faith for Colin, or penance for Tehlor, or . . . or am I a means to an end? Because no one's asked me what I want." She heaved in breath after breath. Talking like that, so quickly, so forcefully, knocked the wind out of her. "I'm nobody," she said, exasperated. "But I deserve to know why you're doing this."

Juniper folded her arms, holding the handle on the paper bag with two fingers. Sunlight skimmed the jewels punched through her wide-sleeved, mauve button-down, and her hip jutted to the side. She looked pensive. Offended, maybe. Her eyebrow ticked up and one side of her mouth curved.

"Colin and I have our differences, but he's still family. Even now, even after losing Isabelle. She loved him, so I love him, and he—"

"Doesn't know me."

"Doesn't have to," she said matter-of-factly, and tapped her foot. "Look, you want to know why *I'm* helping you, Sophia? Because the magic you're carrying could eat a hole through reality and invite displaced spirits to take up residence in whoever's weak enough to let them. Yeah, you're . . ." She stopped, shifting her jaw back and forth. "You're fascinating. You *interest* me."

"Why?"

"Because I've never met someone so hell-bent on staying possessed." Laughter tripped out of her, bitter and scathing. "Sometimes people do things because it's all they *can* do. Sure, maybe Colin's chasing a ghost, maybe the witch is trying to do right by you, maybe I'm selfish." She shrugged, shaking her head. "But fine, I'll bite. What do *you* want?"

Sophia closed her mouth and chewed on the question. Her attention hopped around, eyes landing everywhere except for Juniper. *I want to live,* she thought, but it wasn't quite true. *I want power. I want retribution. I want to start over.* She gripped the charm dangling from the bottom of her rosary. *I want my sister back. I want a time machine. I want to kiss you.* Her heart floundered.

"I want this to mean something," Sophia said, meeting Juniper's gaze. Sunlight flashed across the psychic's eyes, turning them maple. "*I* want to mean something."

Juniper nodded. "It will," she said simply, perfectly. "You do."

Sophia chose to believe her. "Where are you taking me for lunch?"

Juniper smiled and Sophia thought of God, and virtue, and honor, and martyrdom.

Somewhere close, Amy whispered, "The Lord will keep her."

She can keep me, Sophia thought. *Please, keep me.*

"Colin thinks it's too big," Tehlor said, annoyed.

Colin huffed. "It *is* too big. We should be utilizing a small, containable space, not the entire attic."

Sophia stood at the top of a narrow, claustrophobic staircase. A crow shot past the rectangular windows lining the circular wall and each footstep wheezed, echoing toward the cone-shaped roof. She stepped onto the scratchy wood floor. The empty tower was odd, much like the rest of the Belle House, with dusty eaves and blank walls. An abandoned birdcage hung from a white chain near the leftmost window and an ornate Persian rug was rolled and propped in the corner next to the doorway.

Juniper turned in a circle, surveying the room. "We'll all be in here, Colin. Space might be a good thing considering the circumstances."

Lincoln raked his hand through his cropped, dusty-blonde hair. "We sealed the baseboards with runic spellwork, smoked out the ceiling with rosemary and lavender, and oil washed the floor. Should be good and ready for a ritual."

"We put the boxes that were up here in the foyer," Tehlor said.

"Good . . ." The psychic held out her hand, palm upright. "We'll need a lure, I think. Something to sacrifice." Gunnhild scampered behind Lincoln's feet and placed her palms on his calf, peeking around his ankle. "Not you," she assured, laughing under her breath. "I know someone on the east side who can probably get us what we need. Bishop, could you go?"

They shrugged. "Sure. What am I getting?"

"A rabbit."

Every muscle in Sophia's body flexed. "We're not killing a rabbit," she blurted.

"It'll come back with you," Juniper assured. She flicked her wrist toward Tehlor. "She has a rat; you'll have a rabbit."

The witch tipped her head. Her ponytail, anchored with a small braid, flopped to the side. "It's a little more complicated than that, but yeah, sure, we'll bring the bunny back too."

"I don't sacrifice things," Sophia said, casting wide eyes around the room. She looked to the priest for help. "We don't *do*sacrifices, right? That's old-world shit. We don't—"

"Haven sacrificed you, didn't they?" Lincoln interjected.

Sophia pulled her slack jaw shut.

"Your spirit will have its teeth in Tehlor, but a secondary life force will entice your god," Juniper said.

Colin shifted in place, standing in front of the farthest window. He plucked awkwardly at the bottom of his tweed vest. "I understand your hesitation, but animal sacrifices were customary before the New Testament. It seems barbaric, I know . . ." His mouth hovered open. Finally, he said. "It *is* biblical, I'm afraid."

"I'm not doing it," she said. "I'm not—I can't."

"You can," Juniper said. She crossed the room and stepped past Sophia, eyeing her down the bridge of her nose. "And you will."

Hours ago, Sophia had held on to Juniper's waist while they cruised through Little Tokyo. They'd stopped at a tiny, traditional ramen restaurant and sat side by side, drinking Japanese beer, slurping broth, bumping their shoes together beneath the table. Juniper had taught her how to spin noodles into a nest, and Sophia rattled off about her favorite book. They didn't talk about possession, or ritualism, or religion, but they laughed, and listened, and enjoyed a plate of chewy mochi for dessert.

The whiplash—comfort to confrontation—left Sophia unmoored.

"I'll ready the tub for your cleansing bath," Juniper said, speaking over her shoulder before she descended the staircase.

Bishop, Colin, Tehlor, and Lincoln studied her, wearing varying shades of the same pitiful expression. It was Colin who walked toward her, though. It was him who grasped her hand, lifted her palm, and patted her knuckles.

"C'mon, let's go for a walk," he said. "I don't have many people to pray with."

Sophia didn't protest. She followed him down the staircase and through the hall. She tried to resist looking into the bathroom, but she couldn't help herself. Juniper glanced up. She crouched over the oversize claw-foot tub, scrubbing with oil and soap that smelled like an orange grove. Her dark eyes were apologetic, but her mouth was set and stern. Colin kept on, so Sophia did, too, trailing him all the way to the backyard.

Two hawks perched on the telephone wire behind the fence, sleek predators staring at every nook and cranny of the neighborhood. Hunting for mice and moles, displacing pigeons and warblers. Sophia stared at them until she stepped into the greenhouse, greeted by warm, damp air and the smell of soil.

"I wasn't expecting to come back to Gideon and find you," Colin said. His palm skimmed a tall tomato vine roped through a wooden plant stand. "Wasn't expecting a militant resurrectionist cult, an ongoing murder investigation . . . Yeah, I didn't really sign up for any of this, so to speak."

"Sorry," Sophia said.

"Don't be."

"I wasn't expecting a witch to murder my . . ." Her what? Friends, no. Family, technically. "Definitely wasn't expecting to become a . . . a . . ."

"Banshee?"

"Banshee," she tested, sounding out the word.

"Do you want to live, Sophia?" Colin asked, halting before an oversize zebra plant. He lifted his chin and waited, watching her.

Yes. That was the correct answer. The predictable answer. She recognized her own hesitation. Analyzed it. "Do *you* want me to live?"

"What I want doesn't matter—"

"It does, actually. Because I don't know you. I don't know Bishop, or Tehlor, or Lincoln, or June."

"You can't comprehend someone's ability to care for you simply because you're in need of it?" He narrowed his eyes and scoffed. "No wonder you and Bishop get along."

"I can't comprehend a group of fucked-up people giving a shit about me," she snapped. It was harsh and impolite, and she immediately wanted to wilt. "Look, I'm sorry . . . I . . . That's not what I meant—"

"It's exactly what you meant," he said, laughing. "I can't blame you for being skeptical, but I can wonder about your desire to downplay both your affliction and your power."

"I don't have any power."

"You're the lone survivor of a massacre committed by one of the most capable witches I've ever encountered. Tehlor isn't forgiving, Sophia. There's a heart buried somewhere in her chest, I'm sure of it, but make no mistake, you're here because she *couldn't* kill you." He shot her a thoughtful look. "Do you really think she'd keep you alive if she had another choice? You threaten her alibi, you carry the magic she intended to take for herself, and you're completely unstable—"

"I'm stable."

Colin laughed again. "So tell me . . ." He propped his shoulder against a glass-paneled wall. "Why don't you want us to keep you alive?"

"I do—"

He said her name forcefully, like a parent. "Sophia."

"Because I don't know how," she blurted. The truth was a heavy thing, weighing on her sternum like an anvil. "I was destined to die and now I'm . . . I want to live! I have purpose, I have . . ." *Hope.* She set her pointer finger against her opposite palm, pressing on the covered puncture. "I don't want this ritual to fall apart, Colin. But God has already failed me," she choked out. Her throat thickened. "They invoked his name while they drowned me. They called to him, they praised him, while I . . . I was *tortured*. I panicked, and begged, and prayed, and God still allowed it. The Lord witnessed my suffering and did nothing and now I should trust *you*?" She flailed her arm toward him. Sniffled, tipped her head back, and closed her eyes. Crying was exhausting. "I know you're a good man, okay? But I've put my trust in a lot of people I shouldn't have." She pawed at an annoying tear. "Cut me some slack."

The priest inhaled deeply. His shoulders drooped. "Dying would be easier."

"Yeah, it fuckin' would be," she muttered, swiping at her leaky nose and salty cheeks.

"Hail Mary," Colin started, softly, like any good priest would, "full of grace, the Lord is with thee." He stepped forward and cradled Sophia's bandaged hand.

Sophia sighed and closed her eyes. "Blessed art thou amongst women and blessed is the fruit of thy womb, Jesus."

They spoke together. "Holy Mary, Mother of God, pray for us sinners now and at the hour of our death."

Sophia clutched his hand, and Colin clutched hers, and she hated how safe it felt to join in prayer with someone else again. To hold on to whatever scraps remained of her faith in the presence of another person. The prayer lingered. Ghosts whispered. One of the hawks let out a shriek. Colin sighed.

"Someone's been talking to me," Sophia whispered, as if she'd uttered a secret. Maybe she had. "A woman, I think."

"One of the departed?"

"No. She . . ." Her voice wavered. "Judas called her the mistaken daughter."

Colin stared at her for a long, long time, so long, in fact, that Sophia wanted to crouch down and begin digging. Bury herself. Disappear. He narrowed his eyes and mouthed the words back to her—*mistaken daughter*—before his pupils dilated, and he flexed his jaw, and everything seemed to worsen.

He squeezed her knuckles. "Did this happen before or after you screamed?"

"After."

A soft, profound sound puffed out of him. Then he said, "You'll sacrifice the rabbit," and she realized she had no choice. None at all. "Have you ever heard of Hecate, mother of witchcraft? Or Hel, keeper of the Norse underworld?" When she swallowed and shook her head, Colin made another sound. Sharper. The opposite of a gasp. "Persephone, Cerridwen?" Again, she shook her head. Colin tongued at his cheek and leaned closer, touching two fingers to the center of her bandaged palm. "What about God's first earthly creation, so beautiful, so bold and curious, that God cast her out before light ever touched Eden? Before Adam or Eve ate from the apple? Do you know her?"

Deep, smoldering laughter brushed her ear, like an echo caught in a net.

"That's heresy," Sophia joked, because it was all she could do to keep from shaking.

Colin—steady, kind, gentle Colin, who smiled often and showed her compassion—looked afraid. "The rabbit will come back with you," he said, and cleared the fear from his voice. His smile was brittle and small. "I promise."

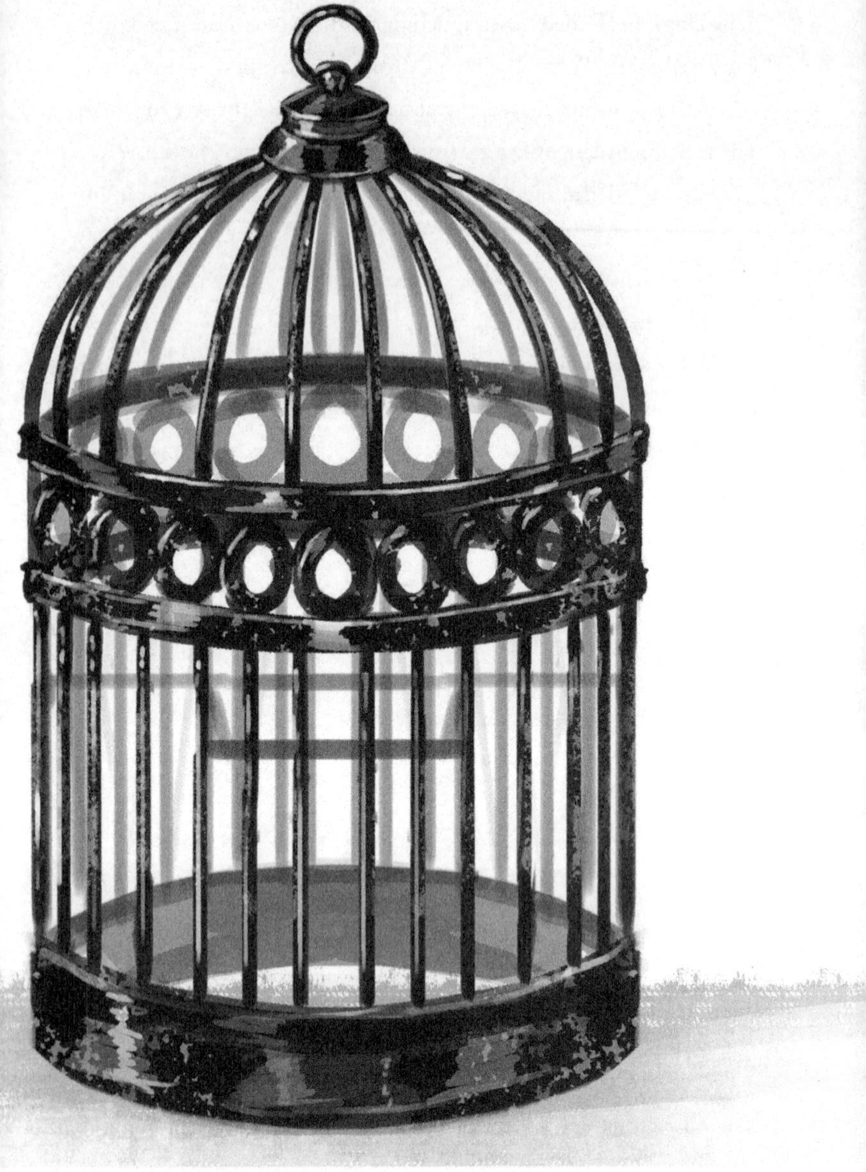

Chapter Nine

"**L**ET ME," JUNIPER SAID.

Evening chased shadows down the hall, causing candlewicks to quiver. Hours ago, Sophia had stood in the greenhouse with Colin, crying and praying, and minutes ago, she'd nibbled orange slices while Lincoln cubed salmon for a stew. Everyone ate in separate places at different times, spooning milky soup into bowls at their leisure. Bishop and Colin ate on the front porch, limned by sunset. Sophia sat at the palmistry table in the foyer, stealing glances at them through the window. She watched them kiss, the way Colin's mouth fit against Bishop's, how Bishop chased him when he pulled away, and realized she'd never been kissed with such surety.

She thought about that while Juniper unfastened the bandage from her palm. A small, round scab dented her hand.

"I'm sorry for earlier," the psychic said. "Forgive me, conejita."

Sophia didn't know how to offer forgiveness for body language, or tone, or attitude. Those things weren't actionable, they just were. "It's fine," she said, and turned toward the steaming bathtub. "What's in there?"

"Salt and stones, mostly. Holy Water too. It'll get rid of nasty energy." She ushered Sophia toward the tub. "Just holler if you need anything—"

"You can stay," she said. The words left her in a rush. "And we can talk, maybe. If you want."

Juniper blinked at first, then she nodded and swiveled on her heels, facing the closed bathroom door. With her back turned, Sophia took the chance to strip, leaving her sweater and pants in a heap followed by cotton underwear and a wireless bra. She slipped her toe into the dark, purplish water. It stung at first, numbness giving way to comfort, and she sighed as she sank below the surface.

"You can turn around," Sophia said.

The psychic sat instead, placing her back flat against the side of the tub, and tipped her head, resting her cheek on the white edge.

"You don't have to be sorry for tryin' to talk sense into me," Sophia said. She reached below the water and fished around for a stone, lifting a toothy amethyst from beneath her thigh. "But I don't think I can . . ." *Kill again.* "I don't think I can hurt a bunny, June."

"We'll cross that bridge when we get to it. How're you feeling? How was dinner?"

"Oh, fine. Lincoln's a good cook. You had some of his stew, didn't you?"

She nodded. "Surprisingly enough, he *is* a good cook."

Quiet surfaced between them and Sophia wished she knew what to do with it. Instinct told her to find comfort in the silence, to resist breaching, filling, or ruining it, but she wanted to know Juniper's thoughts. Wanted to understand.

"You're nervous," Sophia said. The tips of her hair floated in the water, chin submerged, heat and salt sinking into her skin.

"Aren't you?" Juniper met her eyes. She wore an easy smile.

Terrified. "Nervous isn't the right word. I'm at a loss. If I do the ritual, I die. If I don't do the ritual, I die. The Breath of Judas is killing me slowly, so I might as well let you kill me fast, right?" She aimed for humor, but the joke fell flat. "What happens if you can't bring me back?"

"I *will* bring you back."

"If you can't."

"That's not an option."

"It's always an option," Sophia said, leveling her with a patient glare. "C'mon, you're telling me magic is totally, completely safe? That ritualism and"—she wiggled her fingers—"this woo-woo shit isn't just as dangerous as Haven? I know I got roped into a cult, I get that, but I'm not stupid."

Juniper ruminated on that. She turned her gaze toward the high ceiling and swayed her feet, ankles crossed, hands folded in her lap. Her chest lifted on a great breath.

"Ultimately, it'll be up to you," she said, exhaling slowly. "I'll be there to guide you, though."

Before Sophia could speak, knuckles rapped the bathroom door. One second later the knob jiggled, hinges wheezed, and Tehlor swept into the bathroom, kicking the door shut behind her.

"Hey, Bishop took Colin's car to go get the . . ." She set her hands on her hips, assessing the bathtub. "Oh, what the fuck, why didn't you come get me? Hold this." Tehlor handed Juniper a neatly rolled joint and lifted the edge of her shirt, tossing the garment away.

Sophia's chin met her chest. She stared at the water, mouth agape, and tried not to blush. "What the hell are you doing?"

"Getting in. Scoot over," Tehlor said. She pulled a band off her wrist and tied her hair into a bun, then worked off her jeans, shimmied out of her underwear, and stepped into the tub, shooing Sophia's feet. *"Move."*

Bold laughter echoed around the steamy room and Juniper shook her head. Her giggles and cackles filled the space.

Sophia pulled her knees to her chest—*mortified*—and desperately tried to keep her attention on the purplish bath. But she couldn't ignore Tehlor's pale skin sinking into the tub. How Tehlor's feet knocked against her hip and the water sloshed over the side, causing Juniper to shriek and laugh harder. Wet rosebud nipples, and red ink, and sharp collarbones. The witch had no shame. Sophia envied her for it.

"Calm down," the witch yowled. She poked Sophia's cheek with her toe, earning a swat. She grinned and scissored two fingers toward Juniper, asking for the joint. "So Colin told me you've been communing with Lilith."

At the same time, Sophia and Juniper said, "What?"

"Hey, don't shoot the messenger. That's what the cleaner said," she mumbled, pinching the skinny end of the joint between her lips. The tip smoldered and sparked, lighting without the use of a flame. It was things like that, casual magic, that made Sophia's chest clench. Tehlor blew plumes into the air and tipped her head back, sinking deeper into the tub. She rested her ankles on the lip next to Sophia's shoulder. "She's one tough bitch, little girl. Be careful."

"I have no idea who I'm *communing* with, but it's not lily—"

"Lilith," Juniper corrected.

Tehlor laughed.

"Lilith, whatever," Sophia snapped.

"It's not whatever," Tehlor said. Her tone was sobering. She took another puff and held the joint toward her. When Sophia shook her head, she shrugged. "I'm guessing you don't know much about her given Haven's obsession with building a necrophiliac army—"

Juniper whipped around. "Tehlor—"

"What, c'mon, she was there," Tehlor sneered. She offered the joint to Juniper, who politely declined. "But yeah, anyway, do you know who she is?"

Sophia shook her head. She knew Mary of Nazareth, and Rachel—*God hearkened to her*—and Miriam the prophet, and Mary of Bethany, and all the other women scattered throughout the Bible. But the only one she could manage to think about was Lot's wife, unnamed and a bearer of burdens, who glanced back at Sodom and was turned into a pillar of salt. She relaxed, extending her legs beneath the water.

Womanhood was a strange, changing thing, and Sophia found herself apprehended by the suddenness of it. Intimacy she'd never experienced; vulnerability she'd always yearned for. She thought of movies—teenagers sharing bubble baths, young women doing each other's makeup, brides surrounded by maidens—and ignored her shyness in favor of something else. Tehlor and Juniper, trust and ease, growth and newness.

"Lilith is a lot of different things. She's a demoness in some iterations," Tehlor said, muffling a cough. "A Sumerian goddess, one of the mothers of witchcraft, child of Lucifer, blah, blah. Lots of people think she's Adam's disobedient first wife. God gave her the boot for bein' hypersexual or some shit, I don't know, but there's a few old Aramaic texts that hint at her being the first *anything* too." She met Sophia's eyes. Her smile deepened. "So some people think Lilith is the bridge between angels and humans. That God created her before creating light and cast her out of Eden because she was too cunning to control. Pretty hot bitch of her if you ask me."

Juniper sighed. "Everything is rooted in *belief*, Sophia. People who believe she's a demon, receive her as a demon. If they believe she's a goddess, they'll find a goddess. Has she reached for you?"

Sophia toyed with the amethyst, pressing each finger to its sharp fang. "Someone spoke to me. I don't know who."

"Rumor has it, she's the voice who drove Joan of Arc to victory. Everyone called her crazy, but . . ." Tehlor shrugged and laughed triumphantly, billowing smoke like a dragon. "Viva la révolution!"

God guided Joan of Arc to victory. Sophia swallowed hard. Heat still clung to the water, but a chill ran through her, and she sank back down, submerging her shoulders. *Not some demoness.*

"Hola," Juniper whispered lovingly, like someone would to a baby, and lifted her palm eye level. Gunnhild rested in her hand, nose twitching. "Tehlor, did you leave Colin and Lincoln alone together?"

"They're fine," she assured, smiling fondly at the plump rat.

"If you say so."

"Can we get back to the demon, goddess, deity, *whoever*, please?" Sophia asked. "What do . . . What do they want? Like, how do I do this? I can't . . . I don't get it. I don't know what to do."

"Don't get what? How to connect with deities? Yeah, nobody really knows how. We all just wing it and cross our fingers," Tehlor said. "I didn't expect Fenrir to pick me."

Sophia remembered the mountainous shape on the horizon, shadowing the Gideon Preserve. How snow framed its massive jaws. "That's your god?"

"I have many gods," Tehlor said. She finished the joint and extinguished the butt with a tap to the water's surface. "True gods. But yeah, Fenrir came to me in a dream, then accepted my sacrifice at the revival. Flooded me with power." She considered her next words before relenting. "You've probably never done, like, coke, right? Cocaine?"

Sophia narrowed her eyes.

"Taking that as a no. Anyway, channeling Fenrir was a lot like doing somethin' risky, you know? Felt great, felt fuckin' awesome, felt terrifying too," she said quietly. Her expression relaxed and she rubbed the hawk tattooed on her neck. "Power isn't protected. What's given can be taken away. Faith, though? Worship? Dedication? That'll keep you safe when you've got nothing left."

Finally, Sophia thought, *you're telling the truth.*

"What if I don't want power?" Sophia asked.

"Be for real." Tehlor snorted. "Everyone wants power. Even you. Especially you, actually."

"You don't know that."

A ghost hissed. *Now, who's the liar?*

"Power doesn't always look like oppressive control," Juniper said. She placed the rat on the floor. "It doesn't always look like Fenrir, or Santa Muerte, or Christ either. Sometimes it's an exercise in freedom. Most of the time, it's just a choice."

"I didn't choose any of this," Sophia said.

"Maybe you should start, then," Tehlor said. She sighed and pushed herself up. "Choosing, I mean."

Sophia sent her flighty gaze to every corner of the bathroom, but she still noticed Tehlor's slender body, how bone bent beneath her breasts and water slid down her knobby knees—the scar in the shape of a handprint on her stomach. Tehlor took a towel off the countertop and wrapped it around herself.

"Hold on," Juniper said. She stood and grabbed a cologne bottle labeled *Florida Water.* Tehlor closed her eyes and stood still, welcoming a spritz to her neck, wrists, and ankles. "Don't forget your rat."

Tehlor hummed appreciatively and held the door for Gunnhild, who hopped across the tile behind her.

Sophia considered the space for a moment. The walls seemed to slide closer, forcing her to pay attention to her proximity to Juniper. *Be brave.* She wanted to scream again, to silence the nonsensical chatter in her skull. The more nervous she was, the louder her spiritual hitchhikers were. She let a single monumental thought propel her forward: *I could die tomorrow.*

"If Lilith is reaching for you, I wouldn't ignore her," Juniper said. She sighed and met Sophia's eyes in the mirror, still half-steamed from the heat.

Sophia grasped the sides of the tub and stood, stepping out. Water ran from her chin to her chest, dripped from her breasts, and slid past her navel. She was hyperaware of the dark hair between her thighs and the soft pout cushioning her hip bones, but she stepped forward and waited, watching Juniper's gaze flick across her reflection.

"Haven thought nudity was hedonistic," Sophia said. She cleared her throat, lifting one shoulder. "They bought designer clothes, carried around expensive handbags, always had new this or that, but never showed their shoulders or wore skirts without tights. It was subtle, you know? Sundresses that showed too much cleavage were taboo at cookouts. High heels made short men feel weird, so we never wore them."

Juniper's throat flexed. She turned, nodding slowly, and spritzed Sophia's sternum, avoiding the recently magicked handprint at the base of her throat. "Bodies are sacred," she said. Another spritz to each wrist. "Shitty people encourage shame instead of confidence because it's easier to manage. Shameful people rarely fight back."

"I did," she said. The air was suddenly thinner. She didn't want to think of Daniel, of his hand around her mouth, of clawing uselessly at his chest, but she did. It came like a snakebite and was gone just as quickly.

Juniper knelt and spritzed her ankles. She touched a droplet there, tracing the top of Sophia's foot. "That's why you're here." She looked up. How primal and powerful and surreal, witnessing Juniper Castle like that. On her knees, worshipful. "Survival isn't pretty, Sophia, but that doesn't make it ugly. It looks different for everyone."

"What did yours look like?"

The psychic cupped Sophia's calf, just so. Her fingers met the back of her knee and Sophia told herself not to crumble. Not to sink.

"Men with wives at home who had time to kill and money to burn," Juniper said. The side of her mouth lifted. "That's a past life, though."

"Does it ever stop?"

"Does what ever stop?"

"Feeling it. Reliving it."

"The body keeps the score, sweetheart. Heal your mind, care for your heart, forgive the rest," Juniper said. She stood. Her hand skimmed Sophia's thigh. "Get dressed. I'll bring you some tea."

Kiss me, Castle. She reached past Juniper and grabbed the towel off the vanity. *C'mon.* Wrapped it around herself and chewed her lip. Juniper watched her, that same hawkish expression, those same dark, inquisitive eyes. But she didn't move, didn't take Sophia's hand or lean closer. Just watched, careful and stoic.

Sophia turned and left, crossing the hall into her bedroom. Chilly wind ruffled the curtains. She stared at the moon through the crack between the French doors. Its white face hovered above the balcony, illuminating the Belle House and all its windows, secrets, ghosts.

At a quarter past nine, a knock sounded at the door.

Sophia paused in the middle of a prayer. *Fear not, for I am with you. Be not dismayed.* Embarrassment had wormed into her stomach after she'd left the bathroom two hours ago. She couldn't shake the idea that Juniper pitied her. Saw her as a broken thing meant to be mended. Her palm hovered over the doorknob before she mustered the courage to grasp it.

"Hi," Sophia said.

Juniper, dressed in a nightshirt and silk pajamas, held a fanciful silver tray topped with a teapot, matching cups, and a tarot deck. "You're still up," she said, surprised. "I thought I might've missed you."

"I waited."

Her smile stretched. She walked inside and set the tray on the nightstand. "I wanted to offer you a reading if you're up for it."

Sophia hoisted onto the bed and scooted across it, framed by the vintage canopy and beautifully carved posts. Juniper didn't sit until Sophia patted the bed.

"A tarot reading?"

"Chamomile, lavender, valerian root, and passionflower," Juniper said. She filled one cup for Sophia, then the second for herself. "And yes, a tarot reading."

Sophia brought the cup to her lips, allowing the hot porcelain to rest against her mouth. The sensation grounded her. "Okay."

Juniper's charcoal hair was loosely braided. Stray curls fell around her bare face, stripped of any makeup, and her jewelry was gone. Sophia seized the chance to appreciate her like that, unadorned and classically beautiful. She shuffled the deck once before handing it to Sophia and asking her to do the same. Once the cards were ready, Juniper got comfortable, lounging across the bed with her elbow bent, propping up her head. She fanned the cards face down.

"Pick one," Juniper said.

Sophia pulled one from the center.

"Good. Another."

She opened her hand over the deck and closed her eyes, waiting for some kind of force to guide her. None did, though. She simply took another card.

"Last one," Juniper said.

Show me. Sophia sat cross-legged, staring at the cards, channeling something close to hope. It manifested like longing—an ache spreading from her rib cage to her arm, down into her wrist, throbbing in the stigmata scabbed dead center on her palm. The itch to scream, to open her mouth and release whatever magic whirled within her, came and went. She followed that feeling to the very last card tucked and hidden at the leftmost side of the deck. She dragged it across the comforter.

"Are you ready?" Juniper asked. She aligned the three cards and pinched the edge of the first one. Once Sophia nodded, she flipped it, revealing a cylindrical building coming apart brick by brick. Lightning branched the sky behind it. "The Tower," Juniper said, as if she'd predicted the outcome, and tapped it. "Upheaval, change, turmoil. There's a suddenness to The Tower that people usually connect with. Something jolted you out of one life and into another."

Sophia wrinkled her nose. "Seems obvious."

"The cards aren't always known for their subtlety." She flipped the next. A woman seated in a throne, holding a wooden staff, accompanied by a cat. This time, Juniper hummed. "The Queen of Wands represents certainty. She's uncompromising and steadfast, ambitious and relentless. Since she's paired with The Tower, I think she might be leading you away from the rubble. She's encouraging change and strength."

"Could she represent a person?"

"Yes, or a deity." She glanced at Sophia, eyebrows creeping higher. "Do you have any ideas?"

You, she wanted to say, but she shook her head. "Maybe the voice I've been hearing."

Juniper nodded. She ran her fingers along the last card before flipping it. She tightened her mouth, staring hard at an illustration of two people exchanging chalices. "Two of Cups," she said. The statement gusted softly, awestruck, filled with bewilderment. "This is a binding card. It speaks to unions being made. As the Queen of Wands guides you out of chaos and into strength, you find love, or the prospect of it, and step into something shared with someone else."

Sophia recognized that card. Juniper had pulled it in her room beneath the staircase.

"Some people call it the soulmate card, but I think that's a little . . ." Juniper rolled her eyes. "Cheesy, I guess."

Lamplight accentuated Juniper's body, illuminating the dip at her waist. Sophia tried to be courteous, but once again she thought, *I might die tomorrow*, and let her eyes wander. Juniper collected the cards and smacked the deck against her palm before placing it on the nightstand and retrieving her cup.

"You called me tempting," Sophia braved. She paid close attention to Juniper's reaction, how she paused at the top of a breath, how her hands went rigid on the comforter. "Explain that."

Juniper gave her a once-over before meeting her eyes. "You're twenty-one—"

"Which makes me a grown woman."

"Colin brought you to me for help—"

"This isn't about Colin."

Juniper heaved an exasperated sigh and flopped on her back, staring at the ceiling. "You don't *know* me."

"You were in my head, remember? I know you plenty." Sophia hadn't felt a surge of adrenaline like that in years. Her entire body revved like an engine. Blood ran hotter; heart beat faster. She unfolded her legs and braced on her hands, blocking Juniper's view. "Look, I know I'm quiet, but I can read a room. If you don't like me, say that—"

Juniper made a wounded sound, like a painful laugh. "*Like you?* Sophia, I have to tie your soul back to your body tomorrow night. You get that, right?" She narrowed her eyes. Her full mouth thinned. "This isn't about *liking* you."

"You're right, it's not," she said. *Don't freeze. She took Juniper's cup and set it on the nightstand, then she* slid her thigh over Juniper's waist and hovered above her, hands planted on either side of her shoulders. "But I'm going to die tomorrow and I'd like to live a little first."

"Oh, so I'm your last hurrah. Is that it?"

"You're my first," she admitted.

Juniper Castle tilted her head. Her hair splayed around her, falling loose from her braid. She trailed her hand along Sophia's waist and inhaled sharply. Caution held fast to each movement.

Sophia parted her lips and reached for Juniper's hand, pulling the tender touch along her side. "This isn't about liking me," she whispered. "Do you want me?"

Juniper stayed perfectly still. Her silence wrapped around Sophia's throat and squeezed. Denied her vital oxygen.

"C'mon, fortune teller," Sophia rasped, guiding Juniper's hand over the swell of her breast, higher, around the back of her neck. "Stop being polite—"

Finally, Juniper yielded. She pulled Sophia by her nape and kissed her hard. Their teeth clicked, breath came fast, stuttered and swallowed, and Sophia smiled against her mouth, softening atop Juniper's body. She'd kissed a handful of people before, but never a woman. A girl, yeah. Once, when she was sixteen and too lanky, still growing into her legs. But that encounter, spurred by curiosity and doubt, paled in comparison to the hunger she felt for Juniper Castle.

But first they must catch you. Sophia De'voreaux had been caught.

Juniper kissed like she was starved. Her plush mouth parted, and Sophia tasted tea on her tongue, inhaled the hot gust of a soft moan. One wide hand roamed beneath Sophia's baggy shirt while the other threaded through her messy hair, angling her closer. Juniper's chest expanded, and her hips reached, rolling sensually. The hard line of her cock pressed between Sophia's thighs.

"Sophia," she warned, craning her neck to accommodate Sophia's mouth on her jaw, throat, shoulder. "This is . . ."

Sophia pinched the bottom of her shirt and pulled it over her head. She tossed it, cheeks flaring hot, bare upper half on display in the dimly lit bedroom. Speech became too difficult. Stole her concentration. So she opted for body language, shaking her head, allowing her breath to weigh heavy. Sex had always been a fleeting thing. Never generous, always modest and clinical. For once, Sophia wanted to *know* desire.

To take hold of it, to wield it. If she spent too much time analyzing each action, each movement, she'd fall backward into memories, get stuck somewhere in her body, wading through Daniel and Haven like molasses. She took the bottom of Juniper's nightshirt and waited, sliding her thumb and pointer finger along the seam.

"A terrible idea . . . ," Juniper breathed out. She nodded, though, and lifted her shoulders.

The shirt landed on the floor. Spirits whispered distantly, echoes crossing a lake. She ignored them, focusing intently on the woman stretched underneath her instead. When Juniper reached for her face, Sophia leaned toward her. When she rested her palm there, cupping her cheek, Sophia sighed, nipping at the psychic's wrist. They stayed like that, studying each other, sharing breath and warmth and hazy eye contact, until Juniper sighed and said, "You're enchanting, Sophia De'voreaux. Pure magic."

Sophia kissed her again, savoring the gentle stroke of thumb against cheekbone.

An anthem beat to the rhythm of her heart. *Alive, alive, alive.*

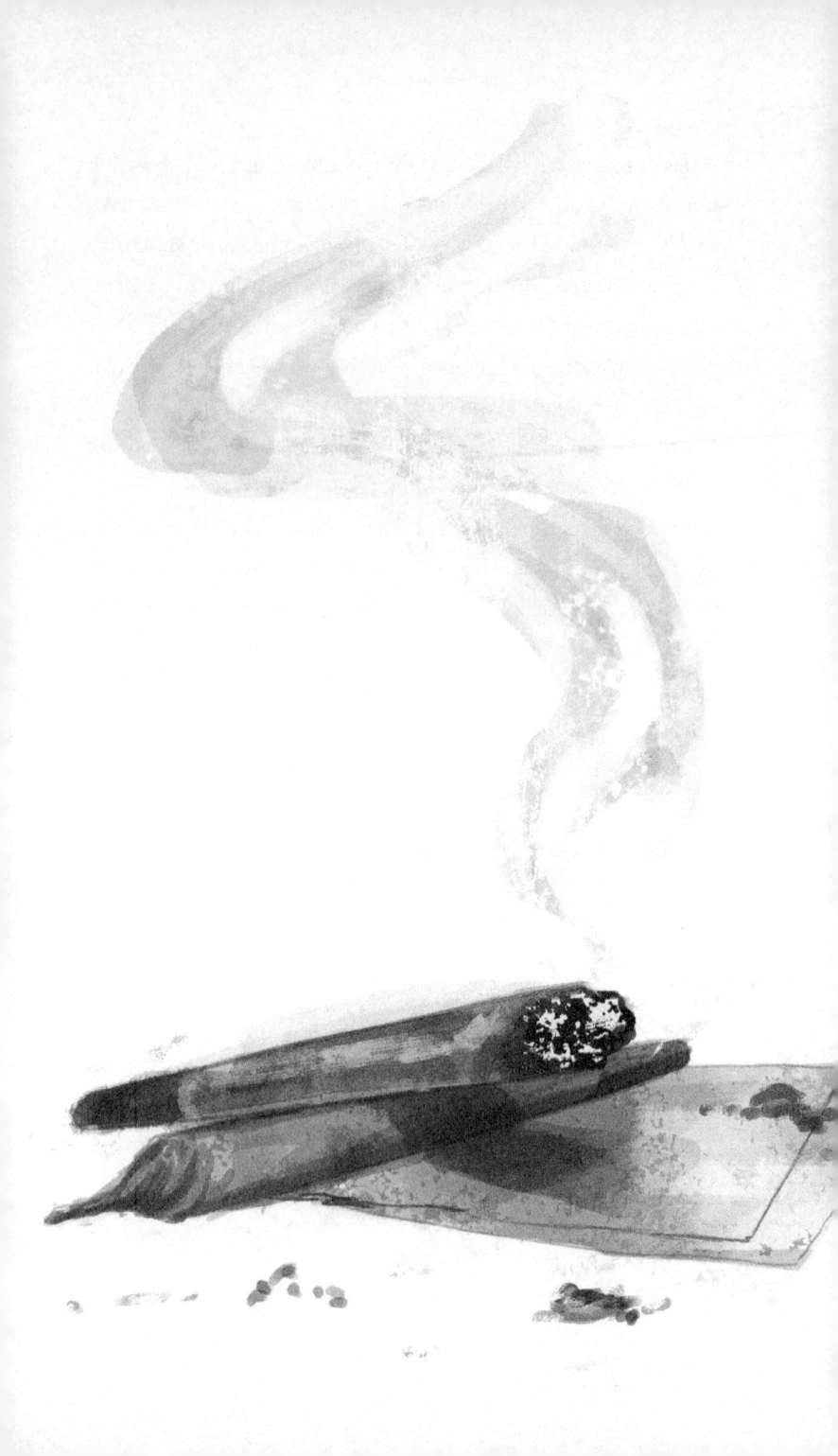

Chapter Ten

Sophia woke to a pigeon cooing on the balcony. The blue hour mottled white bedsheets and cast an astral glow across Juniper's face. Headlights beamed past the curtains, rain pitter-pattered the roof, and Sophia listened to the city stir as Juniper slumbered beside her. The Belle House remained peaceful, enduring the tail end of an impromptu storm. Last night, after Juniper had touched Sophia effortlessly—swept her palms over thigh and hip, pressed her open mouth to Sophia's cunt, gazed at her, awestruck, as Sophia rode her cock, dragging out pleasure, momentum, *everything*—they'd curled close, clutching the quilt and each other, and whispered about mysticism.

They'd returned to one another throughout the night, playing each other like instruments. Juniper's fingers wedged inside her; Sophia's teeth on her hip bone. It was primal: lovemaking like that. The messy, animal kind, overdue and delightfully rich. Sophia felt awake, finally. As if the lock on an invisible cage had been smashed.

Juniper cracked her eyes open. She blinked at first, surprised, before her gaze softened. "Good morning."

"Mornin'," Sophia said. She stroked Juniper's nose with her index finger.

Hours ago, they'd talked about what they shared—natural inclination toward ritualism, fondness for hot tea, love of reading—and laughed over their mutual hatred of undercooked oatmeal. They'd bonded over prayer and repetition, comfortability and loneliness, and playfully argued about establishment and righteousness, privilege and permanence. At one point, Juniper had rolled her eyes and sighed, said *you're young* in one breath, like a lioness scolding a cub, and then smirked, kissed her, and said *come here* in the next.

Sophia pressed her cheek into the pillow. "Never thought I'd wake up like this."

"Next to a fortune-telling lesbian?" Juniper purred.

Unafraid, she thought. *Brave, reckless, satisfied.* "Safe."

Juniper's sleepy gaze sharpened. "Don't mistake comfort for safety. We still have an exorcism to perform."

"Is that what it is? Are you exorcising me?"

"In a sense. We're extracting an unwanted presence from your body. That's exorcism in its most basic form."

"And the ghosts?"

"They'll follow Iscariot," she said. Uncertainty permeated the room, though. "Or . . ." She reached out, following the tendon in Sophia's neck. "You'll scream them into submission."

"I don't know how to scream, June. It's just a . . . a thing that happened. I don't—"

"I'll teach you." She met Sophia's gaze. "A banshee is a combination of two things—harbinger and boatman. Scream to signal the arrival of death, scream to announce the departure of a soul. I can speak to the dead, but you can *move* them."

Sophia shook her head. "I don't think people become magical overnight."

"Oh, they do. But we've trained ourselves not to believe, so when it happens, when we're touched by something beyond us, we call it coincidence and move on with our lives. Like Tehlor said, faith is a powerful thing. Keeps us safe when everything else is gone."

"Faith and magic are . . ." *Different.* Sophia paused, considering. She watched Juniper's expression sharpen.

"They're not," she said, as if she'd reached into Sophia's mind again. "In a sense, they're exactly the same."

"You make everything seem so simple," she admitted. Her face flared hot. "Magic, exorcisms, dead calling, witchcraft, tarot cards—*everything*. Six weeks ago, my life looked like courtship with whoever Rose picked for me, teaching worship songs to newcomers, building an army, gettin' along with the wives. Why's change have to be this fast?" Her accent snuck through, honeyed and southern, like her mother. "Why's it have to be so . . ."

"Drastic?"

Sophia sighed. "Yeah."

"I wish I knew. I think life makes magic out of people who can handle the fallout, you know? Real magic, I mean. Any white woman with a can-do attitude can call herself a Reiki master."

"What do you mean *fallout*?"

"There's always fallout, sweetheart." Juniper leaned in and kissed her, teasing at her lips as she spoke. "There's sacrifice in everything, but natural law is a hell of a thing to break without paying a price. Magic isn't free, you should know that by now."

"How can something I didn't want cost me anything?" Sophia asked. She wanted to bite her. Push her down and climb on top of her again.

Laughter coasted her mouth. "Your humility is endearing, but it isn't true," Juniper said slowly.

Sophia tried to lick each word off her teeth. A voice rose like smoke in the back of her mind. *Little liar on a fire pyre,* the spirit sang. *What is it like to be cooked?* She huffed, annoyed with herself, with Juniper, with the cards she'd been dealt. "What will it make me to stop denying it?"

"Honest," the psychic said, and kissed her again.

The pigeon flapped outside. Rain turned to mist.

I am going to die tonight, Sophia thought.

Juniper slid out of bed and stood on her tiptoes, stretching her long, bare body like a panther. "C'mon, let's make breakfast."

The day slipped through Sophia's fingertips, there and gone.

For the first time since she'd arrived, the Belle House tightened like a fist. Walls crowded inward, fresh air seemed harder to find, and the ritual crawled in with the evening fog, inevitable and thick. Once she'd left the bedroom earlier that morning, the night before became dreamlike and surreal, a thing Sophia reached for as minutes turned to hours. She pawed at the edges of each memory, storing Juniper's half-closed eyes and soft sounds somewhere near the bottom of her rib cage. Away from famished spirits.

Sophia had cooked breakfast with Juniper—crepes glazed with apricot jam—and wandered through the house while Tehlor and Lincoln acquired the last of their supplies. Colin and Bishop had kept to themselves, whispering about *Rome* and *Greyson* and *the Vatican will look after it* as the pair flittered throughout the house. Juniper had kept to herself, too, pressing soft touches to Sophia whenever they crossed paths. Hand to tailbone in the garden, fingertip to shoulder in the foyer.

Evening arrived far too fast, and Sophia folded her arms, watching an orange rabbit with floppy ears nibble lettuce on the kitchen island. She hadn't named him yet, her little sacrifice, and she'd spent most of the day avoiding him. But the creature was there whether she liked it or not, he had a purpose whether she liked it or not, and he would die whether she liked it or not. She touched him for the first time, scratching his fuzzy head. He shied away.

"I'm sorry," she whispered.

The rabbit sat on his haunches and looked at her.

"Oh, aren't you cute," Colin said, appearing through the beaded curtain. He scooped the rabbit into his arms and gazed at Sophia through his lashes. "Are you ready?"

"Is anyone ever ready for somethin' like this?" Sophia asked.

The priest listed his head. He was scholarly and bookish in his plaid, straight-legged pants and cashmere turtleneck. Black ink peeked out from beneath his sleeves and curved like thorns below his jaw. Violet shadowed his eyes. He hadn't slept either.

Colin set his cheek against the top of the rabbit's head. "No, I guess not. But imagine how it'll feel—tomorrow, you've had a hot shower, we're eating takeout around the table, the Breath of Judas is safely contained, you're alive and well. That'll be something to thank God for."

"You believe, right?" She reached out, asking for the rabbit.

Colin handed him over. "Pardon?"

"In God. You still believe?" The rabbit weighed close to nothing, but his sharp claws scraped her arms. She adjusted him until he stopped squirming, supporting his rear with one hand while the other wrapped securely under his front paws.

Colin made a soft, knowing noise. *Huh.* "I believe in the collective good. I don't know if that's God, or angels, or Bishop's magic, or Tehlor's witchcraft, but I've seen more than one miracle in my lifetime, so that has to count for something."

Sophia set her chin on the rabbit's head. "Miracles come from somewhere, don't they? Someone sends them?"

"I hope so," he said, laughing wistfully. "But plagues and curses come from somewhere too."

What's a bad miracle? She kept the question to herself and glanced over Colin's shoulder, meeting Bishop's gaze as they pushed the beaded curtain aside.

"Everything's ready," they said. Their too-big Henley was unbuttoned, creased across their torso, and baggy around their shoulders. They flicked their attention to the rabbit and stepped aside, holding the tassels for Colin and Sophia.

What did *ready* mean? What was *everything*? Thoughts raced by and Sophia found her carefully constructed equilibrium, the balance she'd relied on before the Breath of Judas had split her spirit open, returning like a forgotten season. Fear was a real, tangible thing. Death was too. The irony taste of blood had become too familiar to notice, and the chatter rattling her skull had turned into a constant, droning undercurrent, only fading after Juniper had slipped into her consciousness or she'd conjured enough magic to scream. But right then, as Sophia climbed the staircase and walked down the hall, flanked by

Colin and Bishop, her speech snapped away, flipped like a switch, and familiarity began to manifest in the small, hollow places purgatory hadn't managed to touch.

When death comes closer than usual, thinking about survival leaves little room for anything else. She recalled the feeling of pages between her fingers. Thumbing through that old, ratty copy of *Watership Down* and crying for it after she'd left her mother's house for the very last time, chasing Amy, and glory, and salvation, and Haven.

Hazel, she thought, and adjusted the rabbit in her arms. He kicked his back foot, thumping her forearm. *That's your name.*

Sophia stopped before the narrow staircase leading to the attic. Colin slipped past her, but Bishop paused, too, offering Hazel a gentle pat.

"Está bien, conejito," they murmured.

She cocked her head. Her expression must've been enough to spur clarification.

"Oh, it means little bunny," they said, shrugging. "Darling bunny, tiny bunny, you get it."

She gave a slow, thoughtful nod, and remembered every time that same word had left Juniper Castle's lips.

Bishop gave her a mindful once-over. "Whatever they did to you, it doesn't have to last. You don't have to keep it." They knuckled their glasses up the bridge of their nose. "You lived. *You'll live.* Don't give Haven the satisfaction of bein' their martyr."

Sophia inhaled a quick, stunted breath and carried Hazel into the attic.

Candlelight lit the vaulted room, and an electric lantern sent a dull, white glow across the floor. Tehlor stood with Lincoln near the round window. Juniper shook out a match, talking hastily to Colin, who turned a small wooden box over in his hands.

Sophia halted. The suddenness caused her knees to lock, her vision to shake and blur. Flames reflected off the surface of an acrylic tub in the very center of the tower. It was new, still sporting a price sticker, and looked nothing like Haven's metal plunge tank. Still, she *knew*. Felt the water infiltrate her lungs again. Heard her sister's prayer again.

Hazel squirmed. She readjusted him, cradling the rabbit like a child.

Juniper wore her hair tightly braided. Her blouse was tucked into simple denim, fitted with a bedazzled belt. Dark lip liner cushioned plum paint, bruising her mouth beautifully. She followed Sophia's attention to the tub.

"To undo the damage, we need to replicate the original ritual," Juniper said apologetically.

Sophia hardly heard her. The spiritual warfare splintering her skull worsened. Got louder, fuller, more desperate.

And I fight, not as one who beats the air, but I discipline my body and bring it into subjection. The scripture came from somewhere deep, shouted, chanted, sobbed. Judas Iscariot's voice chimed above the rest. *What a wicked game, to be alive, to die in vain. The tree spoke to me that day. Relinquish your misery, it said, become what is expected.* She focused on Juniper. On the tub. On the flickering candles, and the rabbit's heartbeat against her wrist, and the reflection in the circular window directly across from her.

There, on the night-stained glass, Amy De'voreaux stood where Sophia should've, watching the scene unfold.

"The first thing we need to do is get the sacrifice ready," Tehlor said.

Sophia tucked Hazel closer to her chest. She glanced between everyone, settling her attention on the witch.

Tehlor grimaced and showed her palms. Gunnhild perched on her shoulder. "He'll come back with you, honey. Try not to sweat it."

Colin approached next, holding a small vial in one hand and the box in the other. "I'd like to anoint you in Holy Water before we start." When she lifted one finger away from the rabbit and pointed at the box, he continued. "Forged from the tool that decapitated Paul the Apostle."

Laughter rumbled in Lincoln's chest. "That's the box you thought could—"

Tehlor swatted him before he could finish. *"Leave it."*

Juniper stepped forward, sighing through her nose. "Once we've established the connection between you and Tehlor, you'll make your sacrifice, and the ritual will start. You'll enter the afterlife, suspending the Breath of Judas in your empty vessel, which will give me an opportunity to extract it. Then I'll guide you back. Bishop will assist. Colin will keep the room warded while you're in limbo. Lincoln will siphon energy to Tehlor, keeping you both anchored. Do you understand?"

Sophia nodded. Such simple instructions. Such an impossible task.

I am going to die tonight.

"I'll bring you back, Sophia," Juniper whispered. She met Sophia's wide, unblinking eyes, and squeezed her elbow. "Do you trust me?"

Again, Sophia nodded. The truth, harsher, far more complicated, sat close to bone. *I covet you.*

The psychic inclined her head. "Good. Let's begin."

The ritual started the way all terrible things were meant to start. With the death of innocence.

Sophia held Hazel like a lifeline before reluctantly handing him to Tehlor. Her consciousness, cluttered and fearful, still clamored for the stability slowly slipping out from under her. Tehlor handed her a long, hollow blade, shaped like a needle—horror movie shit, the kind people plunged into eye sockets or pushed between ribs—and gestured to the soft indent on the rabbit's chest. *I can't,* she thought, again and again, like a metronome ticking. *I can't, I can't, I can't.*

But as she lowered herself into the tub, water soaked through her clothes, and she watched the witch kneel beside the freestanding bath, saw how carefully she held Hazel in place. Her pale hands, gentle and sure, lifted him up, and one long, knobby finger stretched toward the middle of his upper half, tapping rusty fur. Her glacial eyes stayed pinned to Sophia.

Mayhem thickened the air. The cloistered magic, humming between each wall, radiated outward from the individual practitioners, churning into an unrecognizable presence. On the other side of the tub, Lincoln removed his labradorite necklace and shook out his wolfish head. Bishop, golden-eyed, mouth shaping an incantation, paced in front of the doorway. Colin trickled Holy Water onto Sophia's forehead and said a quick blessing. Her hand trembled, pinching the silver weapon. She exhaled a quaking breath and urged her wrist to move. Nothing. Water sloshed around her shoulders.

Tehlor adjusted the rabbit. "It's okay," she assured, nodding. "It'll be quick."

I'm sorry, Sophia thought, screaming a silent apology to nowhere, to no one. The spirit world echoed her, hollering the same sentiment. *I'm sorry, I'm sorry, I'm sorry—*

Before she realized what she'd done, Hazel seized and twitched, flopping uselessly in Tehlor's grip. Blood dripped into the water, twisting like distilled smoke. Sophia hardly glimpsed the rabbit's limp corpse before two hands latched around her shoulders—Lincoln—and another landed on her sternum—Juniper—and she was submerged.

Beyond the water, Sophia saw Tehlor streak the rabbit's blood down her face.

At the same time, Colin struck his palms together. A heavenly, powerful gong cracked through the room.

Sophia opened her mouth to scream, but she gasped instead. Water, so much, too much, filled her tired lungs. Death arrived, déjà vu, and peeled Sophia De'voreaux from flesh and bone, de-armoring the soul from the body. She slipped free, glassy and incorporeal. The silence she'd once longed for surfaced in an instant. Postmortem rung, almost, like tinnitus.

But it didn't take long for the quiet to shift, making room for distant drums. No, not drums. Hooves smacking hard ground, growing closer.

The comfortable darkness gave way.

Oh, king of sorrow. Lilith's breath tasted like dried apple, fresh fig, old blood. *This child is mine.*

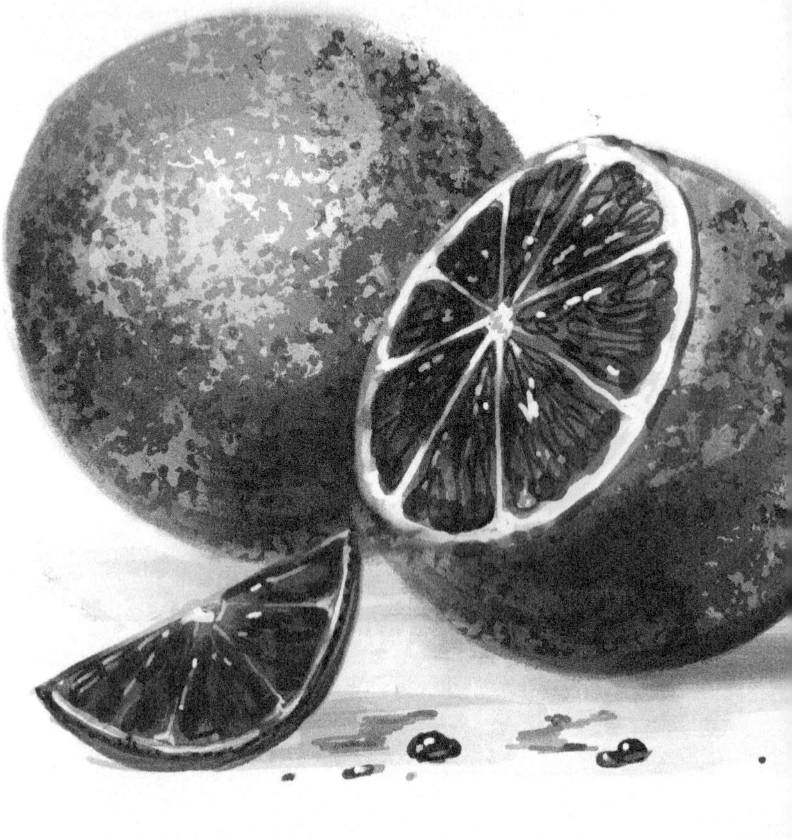

Chapter Eleven

The first time Sophia died, she felt nothing. It was *water, struggle, thrash, no* and *please, breathe, mercy, stop* followed by unbothered darkness and a weightlessness she could not replicate. There was a surety to it that left her feeling unsatisfied. One moment, she'd stared into vast pitch, unable to decipher herself from wherever she'd gone, and the next, her lungs had rioted, and she'd returned. Unmaking murder had been an act of violence. Bringing her back from the brink, deciding against death, was a violation.

This time, Sophia wasn't met with serenity. The otherworldliness split, unfurling around her like a cobra lily, and she stood on a black surface, staring across the night sky, searching for something familiar.

Where am I?

Water dripped from her soaked trousers and her shirt clung uncomfortably. No water puddled beneath her feet, though. In the distance, beyond glittering comet-trails, she noticed light—*firelight*—wading across the blackness toward her.

After is an odd place, she thought.

Unlike the séance, when she'd sank inside herself, death was a place outside her body. Wherever she stood, it was apart from the attic, away from the Belle House, somewhere mortality couldn't reach.

The flame grew closer. Sophia bundled her wet sleeves in her palm and squeezed, focusing on the flickering orange and glinting gold, how cinders glowed atop slender shoulders and singed the end of dark, cropped hair. Sophia's rosary was still fastened around her wrist. The medallion warmed her palm, but she couldn't recall where she'd found it. *It was a gift, wasn't it?* Slowly, the figure became human-shaped and decipherable.

Sophia didn't say their name, but she knew, somehow. Jehanne d'Arc. Joan of Arc. The androgynous saint's eyes shone like polished stone, stark against their milky skin. Flame chewed on them, but they didn't burn, and when they came to stand before Sophia, she expected heat to radiate from their half-melted armor. None did.

Darkness rippled and bent, making room for another meteorite to beam beneath Sophia's feet.

"Courage." Jehanne spoke without opening their mouth. Their voice manifested from above, falling like a cup over a spider.

Something vaguely familiar gnawed on Sophia. The urge to be somewhere different with someone else.

Jehanne stepped forward, turning to meet Sophia's gaze, and walked past her. Sophia followed, swiveling on her heels.

The dark expanse widened infinitely in every direction. Galaxies turned, planets spun, star nurseries gave birth to recycled matter, and Sophia wondered who she might be looking for. What life she could've possibly left.

Death rinsed her, wrung her out, made her new.

Sophia! The call echoed, muffled and grainy. When Sophia glanced backward, darkness tunneled inward, vacuuming out the nebulous.

Hooves, again. Closer. She remembered hearing them before, somewhere. Remembered the tail end of another life.

Sophia, where are you? Take my hand! Take my—

"Courage," Jehanne repeated. Their voice coasted Sophia's ear.

The ground shook. Before her, like a titan, a deity stood on equine feet. Her body presented itself under the guise of familiarity, as if God had opened a deer and spilled its skeleton, arranging beast and human bones interchangeably. Knees bent outward and hip bones concaved, jutting where curves should've smoothed spotted flesh. Above her misshapen ribcage, too narrow, too long, dark nipples flecked her small chest, and higher, slender throat met harsh jaw.

Sophia almost fell. Almost sent a scream barreling through the air.

But Lilith leaned over her, beautiful and monstrous, and wrapped her hand around Sophia's neck, forcing her attention.

"The dead can't be kept," Lilith said. She spoke in a language Sophia didn't know. Arabic, maybe. Or Aramaic. But she understood, nonetheless. "First daughter, first son, first of many. Do you recognize me, girl?"

Sophia stared, awestruck. Thick, curled horns sprouted from Lilith's temples and her slender eyes reflected like black glass.

Sophia!

Lilith leaned closer. Sweet breath warmed Sophia's face. "I have sired saints, I have whispered to warriors, I have stitched ambition into resilient women, and carved impunity out of forgettable men." Her palm dwarfed Sophia's face. When she tilted her head and smiled, Sophia prepared to be swallowed. But Lilith said, "Eden named me forsaken. You will call me *mother*."

Before Sophia could scream, or weep, or say *yes, mother*, something, some*one* reached through the blackness and grasped her wrist, yanking her backward.

Lilith's laughter echoed, growing louder, stronger. *Enchantress.* The goddess hummed appreciatively. Her voice faded. *Fenrir is lucky to have you.*

The darkness ruptured. Something strong and bright caught Sophia's hand.

Tehlor. Witch. *Magic.*

Life—Sophia De'voreaux's life—surged through her, filling all the peaceful, empty places death had hollowed out. The afterlife bent and split. Ghosts drove through the silence; purgatory punctured the deadscape. Sophia came back to Haven, to survival, to fear, to Judas Iscariot and the rot spreading through her abandoned body, to Colin's compassion and Bishop's honesty, to Lincoln's power and Tehlor's friendship, to fate, to an unforgiving world, to a gorgeous psychic named Juniper Castle, to everything.

I will not give up.

She inhaled a ragged breath and opened her mouth.

The spectral noise stopped in the center of her throat.

Amy De'voreaux appeared the same way sunlight passed through cloud cover. *You're different,* Sophia thought. Her long hair, wild and wavy, hung around her face, and her soft, beige cheeks, bronzed by summer, dimpled for a soft smile. Younger. Gentler. Untouched by Haven, and Rose, and Daniel. She thumbed their father's crucifix strung around Sophia's neck and clucked her tongue.

"Take heart," Amy said. Jehanne's voice thundered around her sister's, strengthening each word.

"I miss you," Sophia choked out. "God, I miss you."

Sophia! Juniper called, reached.

Amy took her hand. Somewhere nearby, hooves clopped the starless ground.

All the world will be your enemy.

Sophia inhaled, loosened her jaw, and screamed. The sound started low in her belly and shot through her, rattling the blackness. Amy's unmaking happened slowly. Her ghost chipped away. Bits of her lifted and spun, then all at once, her body flurried apart. The spirits stampeding through Sophia's corpse howled and screeched, but she was outside their hold, disengaged from their damage, and for the first time, she could use the little power she'd found without tasting blood. She sent righteousness into that scream. Deliverance, and vengeance, and apologies. She stitched everything Haven had done to her, everything Haven had stolen from her into the last push, buckling over like a madwoman, like a banshee.

A huge clawed hand rested on her back. Fingers—three bones too many—curled intimately around her shoulders and waist, and heat glowed hot in her chest. Fire licked the rippling dark. Sabatons bathed in flame stepped into view. Jehanne tucked their bent knuckle beneath Sophia's chin and lifted her face.

"Do not be afraid," they said. Their voice was many-limbed, heavy with virtue and confidence. "You were born to do this."

Sophia's scream diminished. Its echo rang and rang.

Blessed daughter, Lilith cooed. She nudged Sophia forward. One hooked claw found her wrist. Carefully, the goddess plucked a taut golden thread. *Burn brightly.*

"Blessed mother—" Sophia yelped. The place where she stood crumbled, and she careened through the pitch.

No, Sophia thought. She swatted at the air. Flailed and twirled. *Send me back, I want to live, I need to—*

The isolated noise from the Belle House increased—ghostly chatter, booming incantations, roaring wind—and Sophia stretched her arm toward it, spread her fingers, reached for that thin, phantom thread until the pitch finally evaporated, and time slowed to a crawl.

Once again, Sophia found herself outside reality, so close she could almost touch it. She hovered above everyone, watching smoke reach upward from extinguished wicks. *There you are.* Juniper stood in the center of the room with her arm outstretched, palm open, teeth gritted. In front of her, Colin struggled to close the lid on Paul the Apostle's wooden box—the prison meant for the Breath of Judas—and on the floor, holding Sophia's waterlogged face, Tehlor sent breath past blue lips.

Sophia glimpsed what they couldn't, though.

Colin was wrapped in unyielding light. Hand-shaped auras reached around him—six, seven, ten of them—all corralling a batch of thick, oily smoke into the holy box. Lincoln, sprawled on the ground, post-collapse. He held Tehlor's ankle with one hand and cradled Gunnhild against his chest with the other. Bishop guided a small batch of humming light toward Sophia's limp form. Everyone seeped, hardly moving. Sophia reached, and reached, and *reached*. Her fingertip met the piece of her soul Bishop had tethered to Tehlor, the part of her waiting to reconnect, and she proceeded to fall.

Burn brightly.

Rich, heady, hurtful life poured into her limp body. She fit herself into every unoccupied place, into every vein and ligament and organ and bone, thoughtlessly rushing through the entirety of what she'd left behind. Time stabilized. Pain bloomed. Sound heightened, sudden and overwhelming.

"Close it, Colin," Juniper shouted. "Do it! *Now!*"

Colin prayed. "Gabriel, keeper of power, ascendent to God on high, I beg of thee, allow the Heavenly Court to extend its might—"

Water spurted over Sophia's lips. A gasp tore through her, chafing her raw throat. Tehlor skittered backward.

Sophia's first inclination after *inhale, oxygen, alive, yes* was to gather a great breath and scream. Power shredded her lungs. The pitchy, whistling sound of a banshee's call—*depart, depart*—sliced the air. All at once, the windows busted, spraying glass across the wet floor. The Belle House shook with the force of it. Juniper covered her ears, Lincoln curled inward, shielding his head, and Colin fell to his knees. Sophia heard the box clap shut.

The scream ended. Silence reigned.

"Sophia!" Tehlor jolted forward. She grasped Sophia's face with both hands, shaking her. The moment Sophia's brow cinched, recognition sliding into place, Tehlor let out a joyous, relieved cry, and hauled her closer. "I thought you were gone! I couldn't find you; I couldn't *feel* you—I was fuckin' terrified. Are you okay? You're okay, right?"

"I'm back," Sophia mumbled. Words tasted chalky, unwanted.

"Yeah, you're back. You're fine," she said, patting Sophia's damp cheek. "Look, see." She gestured to the attic and whipped around to stare at Colin. "Did we get it? Is it"—she lifted one hand away from Sophia and wiggled her fingers—"*sealed* or whatever?"

Colin plopped on his rear. His face was beet-red and sweat-slicked. He panted, nodding dramatically, and lifted the locked box. "It's contained."

"Where's Hazel?" Sophia stared blearily at the ceiling.

Tehlor heaved a sigh. "*What?* Oh, Jesus, the rabbit. Yeah, he's . . . Bishop, where's the bunny?"

Bishop tiptoed over broken glass. They kicked Lincoln's thigh. "Get up," they scolded, earning a gruff grunt from the wolf-man. They waited for Sophia to sit cross-legged and then offered her Hazel, who happened to be very alive. "He's got a strong heart," they said. "I hope whoever listened appreciated the sentiment."

Sophia rested her cheek atop Hazel's furry head. She slid her gaze sideways. Next to the toppled-over tub, Juniper sat with Colin, catching her breath. The Santa Muerte charm rested between her clavicles and curls ribboned her face. She looked back at Sophia and gave a soft, bewildered laugh.

"Sorry about your windows," Sophia croaked.

At that, Lincoln rolled onto his back, set the rat on his sternum, and laughed too. It was barkish and bold. Hearing him like that—alive, relieved, *exhausted*—made Sophia's chest squeeze.

Juniper blew out a breath, flapping her pretty, plum-painted lips. "Easy fix, sweetheart."

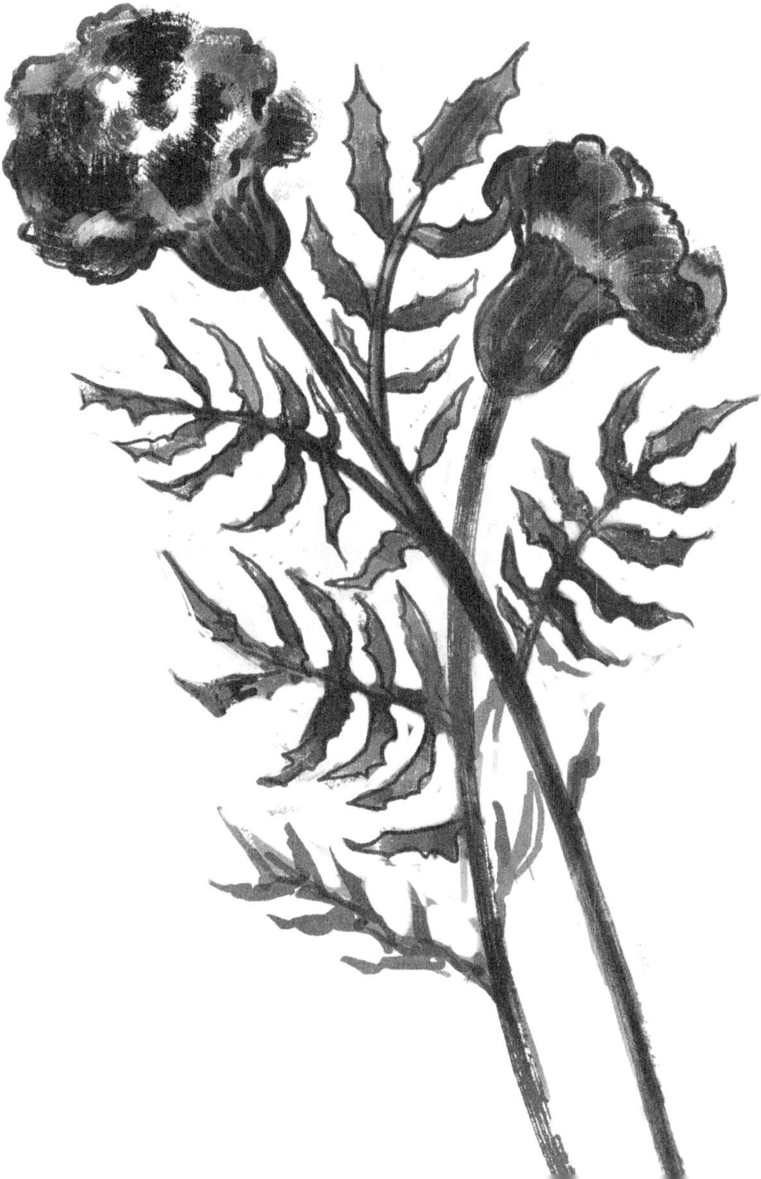

Chapter Twelve

Sophia stared at her distorted reflection in the steamy bathroom mirror, listening to Juniper's *Tycho* playlist over the splatter of water against tile.

Colin was right. Tomorrow had arrived on the cusp of a ripe, pink dawn and the Breath of Judas was no longer sporing inside her. Purgatory remained intact and separate from the corporeal plane. The dead quieted, finally, and her body softened against the breakage left behind. It'd been only a day—less, maybe—but she hadn't tasted iron since before the ritual and she'd been nosebleed-free since visiting the botánica. Returning felt like the frayed edge of an unfinished tapestry, like rubbing a blunt corner between her fingers and watching the fabric split. She was wobbly and fragile, but she was alive.

Every so often she caught a whiff of smoke, though. Heard Joan of Arc's voice in birdsong through the window. *Courage.* Saw a shadow cross the floor, crowned with coiled horns, and thought *mother*.

The faucet squeaked and the showerhead stopped spraying. Juniper stepped around the glass door and toweled off. She reached past Sophia and wiped the mirror with her palm. "Feel better?"

"Different," Sophia said.

Juniper rested her chin on Sophia's shoulder and met her gaze in the reflection. "That's fair. No one comes back exactly the same."

"I don't think many people come back at all."

"True."

"How long did I sleep?"

"A while," Juniper said. When Sophia tilted her head, she relented. "Sixteen hours, give or take." She smacked a quick kiss to Sophia's cheek. "You needed it."

Exhaustion sank to the bone. She swallowed uncomfortably and grabbed the comb off the vanity, swiping it through her hair. The adjoining washroom in Juniper's primary suite was exactly what Sophia had imagined. Clean and cluttered, stocked with an assortment of sweet balms, fragrant oils, and well-loved makeup. The bedroom was lavish and beautiful. White bedding, violet sheets, sun-shaped pillows, and framed replicas of famous paintings. Botticelli's Birth of Venus, Ophelia by John Everett Millais, and The Virgin of Guadalupe by Nicolás Enríquez were among them. She'd stared at the assortment of pinned butterflies above Juniper's bed, clinging to wakefulness after the ritual, hungry for rest but afraid she'd never wake up if she closed her eyes again.

The stigmata mark on her palm was gone. She felt Lilith there, thrumming like a second heartbeat.

"Is everyone else awake?" Sophia asked.

Juniper nodded. "Tehlor's returning the porcelain plunge pool to some"—she flicked her wrist—"athletic depo and Colin's fixing a playpen for Hazel."

"Did we really need to do what we did with the rabbit? I mean, it didn't seem, I don't know, necessary."

"Did Lilith grant you an audience?" Juniper smoothed lotion over her legs, then her arms. When Sophia nodded, she shrugged. "Good. Then it wasn't *un*necessary."

"But—"

"Ritualism is messy, brutal, callous, and old. Maybe it did nothing. Maybe Hazel's death didn't light a way for Lilith, or maybe it did. You're back; he's back. In the end, that's all I care about, conejita."

Sophia remembered a hooked claw snagging gold thread buried in her wrist. She'd felt it quiver, vibrating through her spirit, lifeline to lifeline. That brittle bit of light—sacrificed to entice a god—had been her pathway back to the earthly plane. Her time in the afterlife was dreamlike now, unrefined and hard to reach, fading by the hour. But maybe Juniper was right. Maybe giving life to get back to life was what broke the cycle Haven started.

She nodded and stayed quiet, watching Juniper rake cream through her glossy hair.

They got dressed together. Sophia wore a sweater Colin had gifted her, one he'd outgrown, and Juniper slipped into cool jewel tones, buttoning an azure blouse, and fastening emerald pants. There was an obscurity about it, being alive, being *back*, that made Sophia critical of every movement she made, every breath she took. Haven's mission had failed, but Amy was still gone. The investigation in Gideon was at a standstill, no suspects in sight, but she still knew the truth behind the massacre. Her mother hadn't called; Sophia couldn't imagine a world in which she would. But she still hoped. Everything she'd ever known was essentially gone. What she had left—survival, friendship, magic, faith—was less finite than anything she'd ever chased before.

Every passing thought was a symphony. Loud and harsh without the lonesome, ghostly hitchhikers she'd carried for weeks. For a fleeting moment, she missed them.

Sophia's phone lit on the nightstand, plugged into an outlet next to the unmade bed.

> **Tehlor Nilsen:** curry or pizza

> **Tehlor Nilsen:** say curry

From somewhere on the first floor, Lincoln hollered, "Say pizza!"

Sophia zipped her baggy jeans. "Curry or pizza?"

Juniper shrugged. "No preference. We could always get both."

"Do you have oatmeal and peanut butter?"

"I do."

> **Sophia De'voreaux:** Both

> **Tehlor Nilsen:** big brain

"Can I bake?" Sophia asked.

Juniper laughed, that breathy, sexy sound. It came from her chest, light and airy, and Sophia would never get used to hearing it. "You won't catch me saying no when it comes to you being in my kitchen." She slid a gold hoop through one earlobe, then the other. "What're you making?"

"My sister's favorite cookies," she said, and brushed her hand across the psychic's knuckles.

Sophia had mapped her body, slept beside her, showered with her, but Juniper Castle still managed to make her nervous. It was fast, their genesis, unsettled and new. They'd seen so much of each other in such little time. Trusted each other. Taught each other. A part of her wanted to erase their initial meeting and redo it. She imagined seeing Juniper at the farmers' market. Saying hello as they browsed the same tent. Going out for coffee, or taking a walk, or catching a movie. But Juniper had seen her bloody and raw and disastrous instead.

"I feel like a rescue," Sophia admitted. She swallowed hard, softening as Juniper slotted their fingers together. "Like a dog you found in the rain one day."

"I'm pretty sure that's how Tehlor wound up with Lincoln," Juniper teased. Sophia should've laughed, but she didn't. "Look," Juniper continued, "I don't expect you to stay, but you can."

"Are you asking me to stay?"

Juniper's mouth curved. "I told you I'd teach you, didn't I?"

Sophia inhaled sharply. "Yeah, but I can't just . . . I don't want to take advantage or make assumptions. If this is you being polite and hoping I'll actually leave, I'd appreciate it if you just said that, because I can't . . ." She flapped her free hand with frustration. "I can't decipher it and I don't trust myself to know what's real and what isn't, so." She blew out an annoyed breath. "Sorry."

"Stay," she said, gently, happily, and brought her free hand to Sophia's necklace, straightening the crucifix. "I need an apprentice. You're welcome to get a job, but you'll have steady work if you want it. I'm one of very few five-star psychics in Los Angeles." She winked, grinning confidently. "It's warm here too. I have a garden and a big kitchen. We'll make a hutch for Hazel—"

Sophia stood on her tiptoes and kissed her. Nothing had ever been easy until right then. Her entire life—start to finish—had been dictated by fear, violence, and grief, but this *after*, this origin, this resurgence was an awakening. Permission for Sophia De'voreaux to choose herself. To love herself. To save herself.

Juniper smiled against her lips.

The pizza delivery arrived ten minutes after Colin walked through the front door carrying Thai takeout.

In the foyer, Hazel nibbled chopped vegetables and thumped the floor, staring through the mesh wall of a portable playpen. Gunnhild sat on her haunches on the other side. She sniffed the air, mirroring the rabbit's wiggling snout. Lincoln checked the temperature on a six-pack in the fridge while Tehlor sat at the table, polishing her crystal jewelry. Bishop leaned their hip against the counter beside Juniper, watching her stir cinnamon into a batch of mulled wine. Sophia dabbed coconut oil on an ice cream scooper.

The cookies needed to bake for seventeen minutes exactly. Any longer and they'd burn, bittering the peanut butter, any less and the oats wouldn't soften. She went to work scooping perfectly round clumps and arranging the dough on a baking sheet. The smell alone catapulted her back to a childhood filled with stolen sweetness. Making cookies with her sister when their mother took an impromptu double shift, sneaking soda after bedtime and stuffing candies in their pockets at cheap restaurants. Sophia wanted to keep that. Amy before Haven. Wanted to remember her with peanut butter on her chin, giggling about a boy at bible study, reading fan fiction on her phone until dawn.

Sophia licked dough from the side of her hand and slid the tray into the oven.

"Do you want pizza, curry, or noodles, Sophia?" Colin asked. He placed the take-out boxes on the unused half of the island next to stacked plates.

She cleaned her hands with a rag. "What kind of noodles?"

"Egg, I think. With veggies and chicken."

"Okay," she said, and realized she hadn't actually decided. "The noodles sound good. I'll take those."

Tehlor munched a slice of pepperoni despite fixing a full plate of coconut curry.

The household ate at the table, like Colin promised they would, drinking spiced wine and sharing food out of take-out containers. Lincoln, who had spent most of his energy powering Tehlor's spiritual search-and-rescue, complained about not getting enough sleep before their trip north.

"North?" Juniper asked.

"Canada," he said, shrugging. "Just 'til Gideon quiets down."

"I need to go get my shit first and hire a property manager, but yeah, that's the plan," Tehlor said. She jutted her chin at Colin. "Where are you off to after this?"

Colin dabbed his mouth with a cloth napkin. "Delivering the Breath of Judas to Greyson and then heading back to Gideon for a while, I think."

"Takin' a break," Bishop added, settling their gaze on the priest.

"Greyson's the archaeologist, right? Archivist? Whatever, your brother?" Tehlor pointed at Juniper with her spoon.

Juniper nodded. "He'll take the Breath of Judas to Rome. Vatican City will keep it secure, I'm sure."

"What about you," Lincoln said, sliding his two-toned eyes to Sophia. "Got a plan?"

Sophia spun a wide yellow noodle around her fork. Underneath the table, Juniper tucked her socked foot around Sophia's heel, linking their ankles. "I'm staying at the Belle House," she said, and it felt so true, and good, and real. "Juniper offered to teach me mediumship and I should probably learn how to control this banshee shit, so." She huffed out a laugh, glancing around the table. "Yeah, that's the plan."

"Good plan," Lincoln said.

Tehlor's cheek twitched. She frowned, almost, then caught herself. "You'll visit, though," she blurted. "Like, we'll keep in touch, right? This isn't . . ." She laughed, bright and wicked. "I didn't cover my face in rabbit blood and traverse time and space for us not to stay friends. We can't . . . This isn't—"

"Oh, look at that. Tehlor Nilsen, sprouting a heart," Bishop joked.

She pointed a butter knife at them. "Careful."

"It's never goodbye," Juniper said. The table quieted. "The Belle House isn't going anywhere and none of you are strangers anymore." She lifted her mug. "To a life well lived."

"Salud," Bishop said.

Colin reached over and set his hand on Bishop's shoulder, cupping the side of their neck. "To finding the unlikeliest friends in the most haunted places."

Everyone drank, and the Belle House glowed, and the timer on the oven beeped.

Sophia took a long, deep breath. Beside her, Juniper Castle smiled and lifted her chin, sniffing the air.

What a beautiful life, Sophia thought. *What a beautiful, beautiful life.*

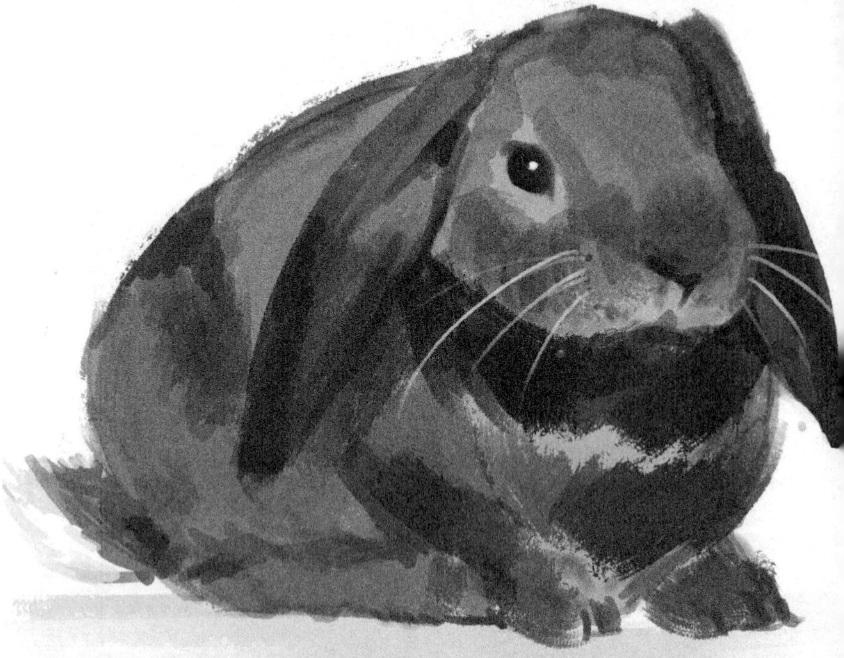

Acknowledgements

I wish I could articulate what this trilogy means to me, but I'm afraid those emotions are too big and too wild. So, I'll keep how I feel tucked away in my heart. Please know, dear reader, that I would not be here without you, though. I can't believe this peculiar story full of faith, resurrection, magic, empowerment, grief, longing, and found family is finished.

To my peers, thank you for your kindness, professional friendship, and challenging conversations. I've learned so, so much from you all. Thank you, Bethany Weaver, for being my industry champion. Thank you to the creators who came before me, penning brave, strange stories that influenced The Gideon Testaments and inspired me to write what I wanted to read. A special thanks to Anne Rice, my queen of vampires, your influence on me is eternal as is your legacy, and another bow to Jeff Vandermeer who writes strange, delightful, terrifying books that told me *yes, you can*—I'm grateful for your work. Thank you to my ever-expanding, voracious readership—you've kept me passionate and excited about writing, creating, and editing, and I can't wait to explore new stories with you.

Thank you to my family, always. You have loved me better than anyone ever could. You make me mighty.

Thank you to the friends who walk through life with me and hold space for me. You keep me in my power when I can't seem to conjure it on my own. I am blessed to have you.

And finally, to the young, reckless, hopeful *me* who had a big, impossible dream and a very long road ahead—look at us now.

To anyone who has ever been haunted by ghosts, or love, or loss, or anything at all: you will find your tether, you will find your way back home.

About ☽

Freydís Moon is a bestselling, award-winning author, tarot reader, editor, and Pushcart Prize nominee. When they aren't writing or divining, Freydís is usually trying their hand at a recommended recipe, practicing a new language, or browsing their local bookstore. You can find their poetry, short stories, and fiction in many places, including *Strange Horizons*, *The Deadlands*, and elsewhere.

https://freydismoon.carrd.co

For information about the cover artist and interior illustrator, please find **M.E. Morgan** here: https://morlevart.com/

Printed in Great Britain
by Amazon